WHAT EVERYONE DESERVES

Dan Ackerman

Supposed Crimes LLC • Matthews, North Carolina

Published in the United States.

ISBN: 978-1-944591-20-5

www.supposedcrimes.com

This book is typeset in Goudy Old Style.

for David

DECEMBER 18, 1952

JUNIUS THOMPSON, known to almost everyone as June, sat in a booth in a bar he didn't mind with a young woman on either side. He didn't mind them either. June liked women, liked them a lot, and got along well with them, though never in a romantic or sexual way. He had never found his appetites running to women.

A murmur rushed through the crowd in that bar and June looked up towards the door to see what had caused a fuss. Last month it had been a fairy, a tall pink man with a funny smile, but today it was only a man and a woman. Vampires, both of them, the man with curly hair and brown skin that was not the dark color that man had been originally but much more than just tanned. The woman did not share his complexion, she was white skinned and reddish-blonde.

In nearly any other bar in New York, in the country, a black man walking in with a white woman on his arm would have caused trouble, but this bar was filled to the brim with unnatural creatures, who tended to pay less mind to societal conventions; not that they lacked prejudices, just that time had taught them not to act on them so often.

The man had his hat in his hand, held over his chest and June grinned when he saw that he had snowflakes in his curls.

"June, you're staring," the blonde on his left, Louise, teased him.

"Oh, he's lovely, we should all be staring," June murmured.

"Don't tell me you're one of *those*," the other woman said, a nasty bite in her voice.

"Don't be dull, Mary," Louise scolded.

"Yes, Mary, don't be dull," June said. "Besides, I was one of those before you crawled out of the mud."

"No need to be sore about it," Mary said.

"Anyways, excuse me, girls, I'll be right back," June said. He stood and walked over to the couple. It would probably be fruitless, but he wanted to at least know him a little better before he never saw him again.

The woman looked at him, eyeing his pale gray horns.

"I've never seen you around before," he said. "I thought I should say hello, as Manhattan's resident demon. Junius Thompson, malak ha-satan, among the first fallen." He gave a little bow.

The woman didn't look amused. "Throwing titles around," she muttered.

"If you're Manhattan's demon, what are you doing in Brooklyn?" the man asked.

"Checking in while Lady Davia is on vacation," he said.

The man asked, "Is there a demon for each borough?"

The woman looked tense. "Is this some kind of interrogation? It is not like this at home," she said with the precise intonation that a native speaker would lack. Her heavy accent gave her away as Polish, but not modern Polish, something older, what a grandmother's grandmother would have sounded like.

"Oh, you'll find the city is a little different than home, considering how big it is and the kinds of things that tend to flock here. My king likes to keep his eyes peeled here in particular," June said. "Come sit, I can answer all your questions."

"Do we have a choice?" she asked.

"Annie, please," the man said, "He's being friendly."

"I am being friendly," June said. He put his hand on the back of the man's arm and guided him over to his booth. "Louise, Mary, I found some friends for us."

"Hi," the man said, smiling, "I'm James Kelly Rosenburg. This is Annie."

"Anastasia," the woman corrected.

A waitress approached and asked if they needed anything. June ordered another vodka soda and Louise had a whiskey sour. Mary continued to nurse her martini. The couple declined anything, which struck June as odd.

"Not thirsty?" he asked.

The man's hand tightened on the woman's slim, white one and she said, "We are vampire, you must have noticed."

"Sure," he said and didn't press the issue. He hadn't been around Old World vampires since he'd left the Old World and that had been years ago; he expected they would have caught up with the times, but it didn't seem to be the case. Severe, stuffy, traditional. He added, "No offense meant," because Anastasia looked irritated with him and James Kelly looked uncomfortable.

"None taken, of course," James Kelly said.

June had to try very hard not to stare at him. He found himself, after a few minutes of conversation, propping his elbow on the table and resting his chin on his hand so he could lean in towards him. The vampire had upturned eyes the color of bourbon set in a face that would have pretty if not for the strong jaw and slightly hooked nose. June wanted to reach over and touch the shadow of stubble on his cheeks. He found himself unable to stop wondering how soft the other man's skin would be. He had not been this enchanted in ages, not since 1247 when he had fallen deeply in love with a young lord who had not cared for him at all.

"So, that accent, you're from Brooklyn, aren't you?" June asked, taking his elbow from the table and leaning back into the leather booth.

"Grew up here my whole life," James Kelly said. "But since I came home, we've been in Manhattan. Annie likes it better, all the crowds, Times Square, the museums. Just home for a visit."

Anastasia gave a terse smile.

"I haven't seen you in my neck of the woods," June said; he knew most creatures in his borough by sight at least.

"We don't go out much," Anastasia said.

"Europe was really something, though. I mean, the parts that weren't...that weren't really bad after the war. Have you been?" James Kelly asked, trying to change the topic.

"Not in a century or so," June answered.

"A century!" the vampire said.

"Sure," June said and gave him a smile. "I've been kicking around a long time. Tell me how it's changed."

Anastasia scoffed. "The people are crass and loud, the women are loose and no one has any respect for their betters."

June held his tongue. He didn't want this woman to dislike him any more than she already did. As a fertility demon, he could pass no judgment on loose women. He ran a pale gray claw over one of his lips, trying hard to keep it out of his mouth. He'd never been able to stop chewing his nails.

He put his hand on the table and said, "You think they're bad now, you should have seen how they started out."

She nodded.

"You were over in Europe for the war?" Mary asked, her fingers running along the stem of her martini glass.

"I was," James Kelly answered.

"What branch?"

"Army."

"My brother was over in the Navy. We lost him in D-Day, he was on the *Corry*." Mary said.

James Kelly nodded seriously. "Sorry to hear that."

"What about you?" she asked.

"I made it all the way through, you know," he said, "When it was over a couple of buddies talked me into doing a tour. You know, Italy and all that. We went to Poland first and I caught pneumonia. Can you believe that? All through that war and *pneumonia* gets me?" He smiled, but it was a sad smile.

"You made it through somehow."

"Annie took pity on me, changed me before I died." He looked at the woman fondly and smiled at her.

She smiled back and touched his cheek. "You were such a handsome face, I couldn't let you go to waste. That skin. Like Swiss chocolate."

James Kelly smiled and June thought that the man's skin was nothing like chocolate, Swiss or not; it was lovelier, richer than any chocolate could ever be, not to mention the wrong shade of brown.

"Do you have the time?" she asked.

He looked at his watch. "Eleven forty."

"You'll excuse us," the woman said. She stood and James Kelly followed suit.

"Thanks for letting us sit with you," the man said and hurried after his woman.

June leaned back in his seat, bummed as the man faded from view.

"Poor June," Louise said.

"Oh, I knew it wouldn't go anywhere," he said, "I just wanted to talk with him for a little while."

"I had a boy like that in high school," she said.

"What made you sure it wouldn't go anywhere?"

"He was Catholic. My mother would have killed me," she said.

June nodded, though he didn't truly understand the division. He finished his drink, chewed his nail for a second before he pulled it from his mouth and asked to be excused. He slipped out the back door, hoping the cold air would clear his head. Maybe it would be snowing. He loved the snow.

He stepped outside and the cold air brushed against his skin. He looked up and saw a dark blue sky with a bright moon. He heard sounds of a scuffle, or maybe lovers, but the noises set his teeth on edge, so he scanned the area and spied a man with a woman grasped in his arms.

The woman he recognized as a waitress and the look on her face was not one of delight. The man had his face buried in her neck and he held on tightly to her, even as she tried to push him away.

June went over and pulled her away; the man tried to drag her back, but June pushed him hard and his back smacked against the wall. Her attacker was James Kelly. June felt devastated.

"Are you alright?" he asked the woman, looking at her neck. A ragged bite mark leaked blood down her dress.

She shook her head.

"Well, what a good place to get attacked outside of, someone will get you fixed right quick," he said, holding her close to his side and bringing her inside, straight back to the kitchen because he knew the cook was a witch with powerful healing spells.

Once he knew the waitress would be alright, he went back to where he had left the vampire, wondering if he would still be there.

James Kelly had remained out back, pacing anxiously, his shirtfront smeared with the girl's blood and his hat crushed on the ground.

"What was that about?" June demanded.

James Kelly looked at him, his eyes wild, blood still on his chin.

"If you're going to be doing things like that, you can clear out of the city, that's not how things are done here," June told him.

"I was thirsty," the vampire told him, a shake in his voice.

"Well, you didn't have to hurt her, thirsty or not!" June said, "You could have killed her. Shit!"

"What the hell do you know? You don't know what it's like," James Kelly said, a weepy note creeping into his tone.

June wrinkled his nose. "For fuck's sake, I wish they'd deal with the ones who can't control themselves," he said. "You're a mess. Where's that woman you were with?"

"I don't know. She went to hunt on her own."

"*Hunt?* What century is it?" June grumbled. He grabbed the vampire by the arm and dragged him through the nearby alleyways until they found his woman with a corpse at her feet.

"You too!" he demanded. "And *you're* too old for this. Two of you acting like you were turned a month ago."

"Mind your own business, demon or not," she said.

"No more of this, keep it clean or you get out of the city. I'm giving Davia your names," he warned.

Anastasia grabbed James Kelly and pulled him away.

June watched them go and had the feeling that Davia would be banning them from Brooklyn before the month was up. He would have to keep an eye on Manhattan, too. He would, at this point, probably call all the borough demons and tell them to watch out.

He went back to the bar and checked in with the waitress who had been attacked, paid his bill and brought her home.

TWO NIGHTS after the New Year, June was settled into his favorite armchair in his favorite haunt. This place was closer to home, only a few blocks away from his apartment and it catered better to his taste in partners though he hadn't been struck by anyone that night. He rested his tumbler against his lips, liking the feel of the smooth glass against his mouth. It reminded him of the times his king had brushed his fingers over June's mouth.

A werewolf waved to him and he waved back.

To his right, someone cleared their throat for the third time, and this time, a voice said, "Excuse me."

He frowned, sat up straighter and looked over to see James Kelly standing beside his chair. "What?"

"I've been looking for you."

June looked him over. He was pale and sweaty, disheveled and sick-looking. "Why?"

"Because of what you said. You made it sound, well, like there's something else I can do."

"Of course there is," June said.

"You mean that?"

"Yes. No one's shown you the right way to do it?"

He shook his head.

June looked at his shaky hands. "How long as it been?"

"Nine days."

"No, since you were turned."

"Seven years."

"Oh, that will be a hard habit to break..."

"But it can be done?"

"Yes."

"Can you help me?"

June stared for a moment, the request taking him by surprise. "I suppose I can."

"If you want something in return, I'll give it to you, but—"

"No, no," June said with a wave of his hand. "I suppose we better get you started tonight."

"Please," the vampire said.

June scanned the crowd, looking for someone who could donate a little blood to the cause. While he searched, he said, "You have to promise to listen to me."

"I will."

He glanced over and said, "And you have to trust me. Trust that I know what I'm doing."

"Anything at this point," James Kelly said.

He had not given the answer June had wanted, but he sounded desperate and June didn't have the heart to turn him away or give up on him without even trying. "Have you got any cash on you?"

The vampire nodded.

"Good." June stood and gestured for him to follow, which he did, with his arms wrapped around himself as though he were freezing. They approached a large man who claimed to be human but that June suspected had giant or something like it somewhere in his family tree.

The man glanced at him.

"Hello, Nate," June said.

"No," Nate said right away. "I'm with Charlie, you know that."

"And I haven't had nearly enough to drink to be propositioning you," June said. "Are you still on the circuit though?"

Nate glanced at James Kelly, thought for a moment and said, "Sure. He doesn't look good, though."

"He's never learned how to feed right," June said. "If you're up for it."

Nate made a face and said, "Alright. Ten dollars."

"Him?" James Kelly asked. "But he's...well, a man."

"Good noticing," June said.

"I don't feed on men."

"You can be picky later," June scolded, taking him by his arm. "Come on."

Nate walked away and they followed him to a back room where they found two busboys smoking. "We need the room," Nate said and the boys took off, sullen but quiet.

June had to almost pull James Kelly into the room. He released him once the door was closed and said, "Alright, here's the rules. You count to sixty, then you stop, no matter what, or if he tells you to before you get to sixty."

James Kelly stared at him.

"You bite where he says you can and you do it nice, none of that tearing throats open shit."

The vampire nodded.

"When you're done, you make sure he's okay. Make sure he eats something, get fluids in him, have him sit for a while. Don't let him out of your sight until you know he's okay."

James Kelly glanced at Nate. "Is that needed?"

"Yes."

"Does he really need looking after?"

"He will when he's missing a few cups of blood," June scolded. "Can you do it right or not?"

"I don't know," he said, "What if...what if I can't stop?"

"I'll stop you," June assured, reaching out to pat the vampire on the shoulder in what was mostly an attempt to comfort him, but also out of the desire to touch him.

James Kelly shrugged his hand off almost the way a spider would be shaken off.

"Anyways, Nate, give him the go ahead when you're ready," June said, stepping back and leaning against the wall.

Nate rolled up his sleeve to reveal a forearm lined with neat scars. He took out a penknife and looked at James Kelly severely. "Here and nowhere else. No teeth. At all. I feel teeth and we're done. Got it?"

"Yes."

Nate drew the penknife across his arm and June watched the vampire come undone, all the tenseness turning to motion, all his defenses and barriers falling as he lunged for Nate, latching on to the cut in a way only a starved man could.

He was starved, June reminded himself in order to banish some of the distaste he felt watching him clasp onto Nate.

June tried to count to sixty in his head but found himself

distracted by the pair. He had never watched a vampire feed with such scrutiny before and seeing James Kelly fall to his knees, gripping Nate's arm desperately with little moans and wet noises escaping him, made June feel strange.

"Teeth," Nate said when June had counted to twenty.

James Kelly did not stop.

Nate put his penknife to the vampire's neck and said, "*Teeth.*"

June rushed forward, knowing that Nate wasn't fooling around. He pulled the vampire off of Nate, holding him firmly, not trusting him at all.

James Kelly strained against him, his bourbon-colored eyes fixed on Nate's arm.

"Did he get you bad?" June asked.

"No."

"Please, I won't, let me finish, please," James Kelly pleaded breathlessly.

"What do you say, Nate? Give him a second chance?" June asked.

Nate pressed his lips together.

"It's his first time."

"Last chance," Nate said. "And you hold on to him."

June nodded. He loosened his grip on the vampire, who was on Nate's arm in a moment, licking up the blood that had dribbled down towards his wrist, then putting his mouth over the cut again. June kept a hold on him, one arm around his chest; he could feel his heart thrumming.

"Time," he said softly once he had reached sixty.

The vampire continued to swallow, his throat moving steadily.

June pulled him back, trying to be gentle, but needing to manhandle him a little to get him off.

"Please," he begged.

"No more," June said, "Not right now." June released him and said, "Go on, pay him."

James Kelly had his eyes fixed on Nate's arm.

June sat him on a pile of boxes and tended to Nate's arm, covering the cut with a clean handkerchief from his pocket and whispering a spell over it.

Nate recoiled at the spell. "What was that?"

"What I use for birth pains, but littler," June said.

"Feels funny."

"I thought it would help. You sit, too," he said, helping Nate over to a seat. "Everybody catch your breath, then we'll get Nate something to drink and eat."

He glanced over at James Kelly and saw that he was still staring at Nate and that he was whispering to himself.

"Maybe we'll get you set up first," June said to Nate, not knowing if James Kelly would be settled and ready to rejoin the world anytime soon. He took out his wallet, tucked a twenty into Nate's pocket and said, "Come on, Maisie'll fix you up with oatmeal and some juice."

He walked Nate out of the room, told the vampire to stay put and locked the door because he didn't trust him. He got Nate taken fed and looked after, then said, "Thanks."

"Don't thank me too much, I'm regretting it," Nate said.

"Oh, he gnawed on you a little, it wasn't so bad."

"He needs help. A lot. He's got it bad."

"If he was that bad, he would have really hurt you."

"You locked him in the room."

"Shh," June said. "You feeling good enough now?"

"Yes."

"Promise?"

"Yes."

"Good man," June said, patting Nate on the arm. "Say hi to Charlie for me."

Nate nodded.

June headed back to the room, undid the lock and found James Kelly sitting on the floor near the door. "Were you trying to get out?"

The vampire nodded guiltily.

June closed the door and sat beside him. "You didn't count to sixty."

"I didn't care. As soon as I smelled the blood, I didn't care."

"I noticed. You didn't seem to have a problem with him, though."

"What?"

"All that about not feeding on men."

"I don't."

"Well, then what would you have done to a girl!" he asked. "Your woman, uh....?"

"Annie."

"She makes a kill every time she feeds?" he asked.

James Kelly nodded.

"That's no good. You're going back to her?"

"Of course I am."

"How are you going to quit killing if she's not? Will she support you?"

"I can do it."

June didn't think he could; seven years of heady, heart-hammering kills would be enough to get anyone badly addicted.

"I'm still thirsty."

"Give your body time to settle, we'll get you more if you need it."

"Please," he said, fixing his eyes on June, his lips parted and moist with blood and spit. June wanted to kiss him. "A little more."

"No begging," June said. "And no more of this starving yourself. A few mouthfuls from a few throats every night or so should be enough for you. It's enough for everyone else. Take some time to relax."

James Kelly swallowed and nodded. He pulled his knees close to his chest and rested his head on his knees. "I can't," he whispered into his lap.

June sighed, straightened up and thought for a while. "Would you ever give it to a girl who didn't want it?"

James Kelly sat up rigidly. "Excuse me?"

"You wouldn't hold a girl down and make her do anything, would you? You wouldn't keep holding her if she said to stop?"

"What's any of this got to do with anything?" he demanded, his face darkening.

"Think of it like that," he said. "This blood thing. It's a lot like fucking, innit? Stopping before the kill is like stopping before you come. You got to pull out quick, you can't push right to the edge, before you get too excited."

The vampire looked sick.

"Stop with that look, you were in an army, weren't you? In all my years, I've never heard anyone talk dirtier than a soldier."

"My parents raised me better."

"Alright, well, anyways, you understood what I meant, didn't you?" June asked. "I mean...no, I won't ask, you'll get mad at me."

"Good."

"Are you feeling like you can give this another go without me having to pull you off?"

"Yes."

June nodded and stood. He reached out to help him to his feet and said, "We'll find someone else on the circuit then send you home. I'll have a better list in a few days."

James Kelly said nothing.

After a few minutes combing through the bar, they found another person willing to sell their blood. The vampire did no better than he had with Nate and once he had calmed for a second time, June sent up on his way home with an address to meet at tomorrow and the feeling that James Kelly would kill someone on the way home.

JANUARY 25, 1953

JUNE DID not think of himself as needy, but he found himself reconsidering the idea as he paced outside his apartment building, where he had been meeting up with James Kelly for a month. The vampire had never wanted to come inside the building and had seemed put off when June had told him he lived within, but the demon hadn't known where else to wait.

Every other night at nine, James Kelly would come and June would bring him to feed on someone, always watching carefully to make sure he wasn't ravaging people. It had been hopeless so far, but June told himself that a seven-year habit need more than a few weeks to set straight.

And, if he was going to be honest, he just wanted to see the vampire.

He looked at his watch and saw that forty-eight minutes had ticked past while he waited. He would give it until ten, he decided, then go in a call Davia to see if she had needed to deal with any unruly vampires.

He waited outside until quarter past ten and had been reduced to sitting on the stoop, wondering why he couldn't go inside. It was cold, the stoop was damp and the air smelled clean and wet, like sleet or heavy snow was on the way.

At ten thirty-something a figure shuffled up the street and June looked up. He stubbed out his cigarette when he realized who approached.

"That you?" he asked, even though he recognized the vampire.

"I'm sorry," James Kelly said.

"Kept me waiting an hour and a half, you ought to be sorry," he said, standing up. The seat of his trousers was wet and he shuffled his leg to see if he could unstick the fabric without being ill-mannered.

"I'm so sorry."

"Alright, well, we've got places to be," he said, coming down the stoop and seeing that he had blood smeared from his mouth down his shirt and all over his hands. "Shit. Oh, fuck! You didn't."

The vampire began to weep, covering his hands with his face and getting more blood on himself.

"Get inside before someone sees you," June said, grabbing him and pulling him up the stairs. He pushed him through the door and after two flights of stairs, he froze up and had to be tugged into the hallway and into June's apartment, a tidy one bedroom that he shared with a cat named Gordon that came and went as he pleased.

"Go wash up," June said, pointing towards the bathroom.

James Kelly stared at him.

June took him by the hand and guided him to the bathroom. He slipped off the vampire's jacket and found it tacky with blood around the cuffs. He tossed it on the floor and started to unbutton James Kelly's shirt. After loosening the tie and undoing three buttons, the vampire jerked back.

"No," he said.

"Then do it yourself," June said and turned away, twisting the faucet taps to get the water warm. He set a washcloth and a bar of soap on the edge of the sink and walked away. He stripped off his own soggy clothes and changed into a pair of dry pajamas and a bathrobe.

He returned to check in on the vampire and found him stripped to boxers and an undershirt. He was scrubbing his face so hard that his skin had gone reddish.

"Hey," June said gently.

The vampire flinched. "What?"

"You doing alright?"

"Yes."

June looked at him for a moment, wondering how soft his skin would be, wanting to kiss his coiled hair.

"I don't want any funny business from you," James Kelly

warned. "I don't care what you do in your own time, but I don't mess with that."

"I wouldn't do anything you didn't let me."

"I don't *want* you to do *anything*," James Kelly growled.

"Then you won't get anything from me," June said to pacify him. He couldn't keep a smile off his face and said, "Not unless you ask."

The vampire really snarled then and June laughed.

"I'm just fooling. Come on, dry off, I've got a change for you. You can tell me what happened and make me understand why you went and messed up."

James Kelly drained the sink, glanced at his bloodied clothes and checked his face in the mirror. He shambled into the living room. June handed him a set of pajamas and sat on the couch.

He turned his eyes away as James Kelly got dressed and said, "Come sit and tell me what went wrong. I thought...well, you know, I thought, at least, you were holding out between our meetings."

"I..."

"You know what, first things first. Was it clean? I mean, somewhere hidden?"

He nodded.

"Alright, good. Better, at least. So?"

The vampire fidgeted for a while, agitated, then came out with, "I shouldn't have done it, I know, so you don't have to tell me!"

"Ho, now, I don't think you've got any cause to yell at me like that. You came to me then and you came to me know. I'm trying to help you. Like you asked me to."

James Kelly rubbed his face, ran his hands through his hair. "Annie...she wanted to know what I was spending money on. And why I hadn't been going out with her to hunt. I told her the truth."

June waited patiently, but no more of an answer came. "Say, do you want a cup of coffee or something?"

"I don't drink coffee."

"Tea? Milk? I might have juice."

A frown spread across the vampire's face. "Are you trying to be funny?"

"No."

"Then why are you offering me things I can't drink?"

"What do you mean?"

"I'm a vampire!"

"I know. Have you been living on nothing but blood for all

these years?"

A blank stare was all the answer he got.

"I'm really starting to wonder about this girl of yours," June said and got up, heading towards the kitchen. He brewed some coffee, glanced back at the vampire and mixed his the way he mixed his own: whole milk, a pinch of salt and a dash of vanilla. He looked at the vampire again and added a spoonful of sugar.

He brought the mugs over and practically had to push one into the vampire's hands. "Try it."

He watched as James Kelly took a careful sip and June grinned when he smiled, his weary, scrubbed-raw face lighting up.

"You promise it won't make me sick?"

"You'll be fine."

They sat quietly together until James Kelly finally said, "Annie thinks that it's stupid, to try to go without killing. That it's impossible."

"Old World," June scoffed.

"But you're old, too."

"Sure but when I first came to earth...I mean, we're talking mud huts and caves. You learn to adapt. Besides, this isn't...it's not my home. Not like it's your home."

"When you said...among the first fallen? You said it like a title."

The vampire was clearly avoiding his own story, but June didn't mind talking about himself. "It is a title. The first who fell was my king. The first fallen fell with him, the ones who supported him. There's the second fallen, those who were kicked out for not taking sides. Everyone else...well, they're the rabble. Not that you heard it from me."

"And when you say your king?"

June smiled. "Well, who else?"

"I don't like guessing games."

"Satan."

"Is that what the horns are for?"

"No. The horns are for fertility. I mean, that's what I do. Make things fertile." He gestured to the two dozen plants placed throughout his apartment, all of them lush and abundant. "Things grow around me, babies come out healthy, girls get pregnant."

"Oh."

June nodded.

"Annie brought someone home. She wanted to share."

To avoid rolling his eyes, June took a sip of his coffee.

"And I didn't want to. I told her. But...she talks me into things." James Kelly hesitated. "I really...I've started to think that she likes it when I kill people."

June nodded. He didn't want to interrupt, but felt compelled to ask, "Do you like it when you kill people?"

"No!"

"Mm."

"I don't! I can't do this anymore. I can't keep killing people. I can't," James Kelly said. "And if I can't stop..." He rubbed his face and ran his hands through his hair, mussing it badly. "If I can't, I have to...and I don't want to die. But I know it's not right."

"We all have our rough spots," June soothed.

They both sipped their coffee.

"Are you going home?" the demon asked.

"After I bolted on her like that? No, she needs time to cool down."

"Listen, if she's got you doing things you don't like..."

"No, she just needs to come around. If it's hard to stop after seven years, imagine how hard it is for her."

"She's got to want it, James Kelly. You can't help people who don't want to change," he reminded.

"She'll come around. You don't go around saving people with pneumonia if you don't have a heart."

June nodded. "Have you got a place to go?"

He shrugged. "I do."

"Do you want me to call you a cab?"

"It might be a good idea."

"Or...it's late," June said. "You can stay here."

The vampire bristled a little.

"No funny business. Take the couch. Just you and the plants. And maybe the cat. You can even shove a chair under my doorknob if you're that worried about me sneaking out to ravage you in the night."

"I guess that would be fine."

June nodded. "Are you done with that?"

James Kelly handed over his coffee mug and June deposited them both in the sink. He returned to the living room with blankets and a pillow.

"Clean and everything," he said when he handed them over.

"Thanks." After a moment, as June had started to walk away,

he said, "Listen, I don't mean to give you a hard time."

June raised his eyebrows.

"About. Being a, uh. A homosexual."

June laughed. "If you think you're giving me a hard time, you should listen to what that McCarthy fellow has to say."

"I don't mean any offense or anything, is all I'm trying to say. It's just...not what I'm interested in, any of that stuff."

"Like I said, I wouldn't do a thing without your say-so. Anyways, goodnight. We'll get you home in the morning."

James Kelly said, "I can't go out when the sun's out."

"For the love..." June sighed. "No wonder you're all messed up. I'll see you in the morning."

He turned away before the poor fool could tell him anything else, maybe ask for a coffin or make sure there wasn't too much garlic lying around. June slept soundly that night with Gordon on his legs, unbothered by thoughts of anything.

In the morning, he wandered into the living room and looked at the vampire for a minute or so, thinking that he looked upset, even asleep. He looked at the clock. He had slept later than usual. He went over to the couch, put a hand on James Kelly's shin and gave a gentle shake.

The vampire stirred, opened his eyes and pulled his leg back quickly, a disgusted, almost sick look on his face.

June took his hand back immediately, his chest feeling achy for a moment. He watched James Kelly push himself upright and pull his legs and blankets in close to his chest.

"What's that face for?" June asked, trying not to sound hurt.

"Sorry, I...I had a dream I didn't care for," James Kelly said, sounding sincere enough. He rubbed his eyes and looked around.

June walked over to the window and pulled open the curtains.

The vampire flinched at that as well and June said, "See, no bursting into flames. I'm not saying to go sunbathing, you'll get an awful headache and probably a little rashy."

James Kelly went to stand beside June, their shoulders brushing as he pressed close to the window, moving the curtains further apart. He stared out the window like a kid would look at a puppy.

"Seven years," he murmured. "You think, what do I want more, to live or see the sun again? I wish I'd picked the sun."

June stayed still, worried that if he moved too suddenly he'd make the vampire jump again.

"I wish I'd picked anything but all this killing..." he said, touching the window. "I mean, I left home spring of forty-two and it feels like it's been nothing but killing and dying since then."

"Did you go on purpose?" June asked. "I know there was a big ruckus after that business in Hawaii."

"You know...all the things they were doing to Jewish folks over there. The rumors, the people going missing..."

"Sure."

"Well, I figured it was the right thing to do. To go over there, try to help fix things. It felt like the right thing to do," he said. "It felt right all the way up until we were supposed to fire at people."

June nodded.

"And by then, you know, it's too late. You can't go home. And, really, someone had to help those folks out. Finding out what was really happening..."

"It was bad and that's mild," June said.

James Kelly looked at him. "Bad? That's all you've got?"

"It's been a long time since things were good for the Jews. Enslaved, dominated, persecuted, hunted, burned. It was a horror, but I can't say it was a surprise," he said. "Do you know what the witch hunts were really about? Other than putting women in their place. I mean, you all—you are Jewish, right?"

"Yes."

"Thought so. Anyways, you all killed Christ and everyone's been awful riled since then." He hoped his tone conveyed dark humor and not conviction.

"Why do you talk like that, anyways? You're supposed to be some kind of demon, why do you put on that Southern accent?"

"I spent fifty years in Georgia, I suppose it rubs off on a body."

"You sound foolish," James Kelly said and walked away from the window. He stood near the couch.

"Anyways, you can go on into the bathroom and shower if you want to clean up. I'll bring you home, in case all this sunlight is too much."

"I don't need you to bring me home."

"Alright, well, do you want a change of clothes or do you prefer the pajamas?" he said. "And, hey, what do you think about blue jeans? I see kids, you know, young people wearing them around sometimes. Better than all this flannel wool. Everyone dresses the same!"

"I don't care much what other people wear."

"Get washed up, come on," he said, "I'll make some coffee.

You want some?"

"Please."

June made and drank his coffee, then pushed a mug towards James Kelly when he came out of the bathroom. He showered and dressed in trousers and a cardigan and lent some clothes to the vampire.

"You get this back to me, now, or I'll come find you."

"Don't," he said.

"You want your clothes or should I toss them down the incinerator shoot?"

"Burn them."

June walked him out of the building and said, "And no more slipping up. See you in two nights?"

James Kelly nodded. "Thanks."

June watched him walk away until he turned a street corner and went from view. He went upstairs and threw the clothes down the shoot, all stuffed into a paper bag.

TWO NIGHTS later, James Kelly arrived outside June's apartment on time with a paper bag in hand. He held it out to June, who peeked inside.

"They're clean."

"Thanks. You mind if I run them inside? You can come up."

"I'll wait," he said and took a pack of cigarettes from his pocket.

June hurried and returned before he had finished his cigarette. He stared at him smoking and James Kelly asked, "Do you want one or something?"

"No."

"So quit staring."

"Sorry," June said and, to cover up his staring, lied, "Just trying to puzzle if you've been ripping any more throats open."

"No," the vampire said shortly.

June smiled. "Glad to hear it. We can walk to our first stop," he said and set off up the block. He took a slip of paper from inside his pocket and said, "This is the circuit I've got set up for you. Two every other night. Names and addresses and everything. And you know, I think maybe in a few, maybe six, months you could be down to once a week or so."

The vampire's mouth turned down at the corners.

"I know, it doesn't seem like enough, but that's because you're used to this pendulum swing. Starving and gorging. It's not healthy. Your body will settle once you keep it fed the right way for a while.

Don't shake your head."

"Annie says—"

"You know, don't take this too personally, but I don't trust your girl. She's got something else going on, keeping you away from light and food and only teaching you to kill."

"You watch what you say about her."

"I'm not trying to say anything about what you and her have going on, I just, you know, I think she's not telling you things you should be told."

"I didn't come here to talk about relationship troubles with you."

June wanted to, but did not, point out that he had as much as admitted that they were having trouble. Instead, he said, "Anyways, once you start letting go on your own, I'll be out of your hair."

James Kelly gave a curt nod.

They walked up four blocks and over six in silence, no sound but their footsteps. June reasoned that it would be better to get away from him sooner, before he got too comfortable. He found James Kelly attractive, but in a way that was more than just looks. He liked him and wanted to be liked in return and he didn't know how soon he would try to start making James Kelly like him.

He would make a fool of himself if he tried to do that, trying to get something out of someone who saw him as a means to an end, who would never be even friends with him.

When he glanced towards the vampire, they caught eyes and James Kelly looked away quickly, casting his gaze towards the ground.

"Anyways," June said, "It's the next building."

They rang and were allowed inside. They climbed to the top floor and knocked on the door that June's list specified.

A woman answered, middle-aged and Asian.

"Elizabeth?"

She appraised them and said, "I didn't sign up for two."

"No, sorry," June said, "I'm just here to keep an eye out. Nothing to worry about, course, he's just new at this."

She nodded and let them in. She rolled up her sleeve, eyed the anxious, eager way James Kelly looked at her and said to June, "Is he good with biting?"

"Uh...might get messy."

She turned, went to her kitchen and came back with a knife. She held it out to June and he stared at it for a moment before taking it.

"I'm no good with things like that." She pointed to a spot on her arm. "Right here."

He took her arm and pulled the blade across the spot she had designated. Her face remained blank the whole time. June stepped back and James Kelly moved in, burying his face in the crook of her arm, his mouth latched on with intense need.

June tried not to stare too much because it made him feel warm to watch the vampire feed so eagerly. It sent sordid images through his mind and made him wonder how eagerly he could put his mouth to use for other things.

Ridiculous, he reminded himself.

He glanced down at his watch and saw that fifty seconds had gone by; he had started wearing a watch just for these outings.

"Time," he called.

James Kelly made a sound that was part-moan, part-whine; June gave him a moment to pull back on his own, but when he didn't, he placed a hand on his shoulder. With that touch, he released the woman and even leaned against June, his back against June's chest.

The vampire's heart thrummed in his body and his breathing came quickly.

"You sit," June said, "Get your head together." He reached up and squeezed James Kelly's shoulder and the vampire languidly pulled away from him, moving slowly towards the couch.

June found the kit the woman had left out and bandaged her arm. "Does it hurt?" he asked.

She shook her head.

He had her sit as well and knew he should make James Kelly take more responsibility for aftercare, but he was so clearly lost in himself, in the blood.

He prepared the woman something to eat and drink and vowed that he would start making the vampire help. As he set the plate before her, he heard a baby start to fuss.

The woman started to stand and he said, "I don't know if holding babies after blood loss is such a good idea."

She still tried to stand. "I can't leave him crying, the neighbors will start to complain about us again."

"Really, I can check on him."

"Bring him right out to me."

He went and found a baby, about six months, getting worked up in his crib. The baby was wet and he wondered if it would be too forward to change this woman's child. He took the baby and went back to the living room.

"He just needs a change," he said. "Which is not outside my capabilities. You should be eating that."

She hesitated but after she looked at him for a moment, she nodded. June had expected as much; mothers usually trusted him with their children and children tended to enjoy his company. He changed the baby, held him for a moment, soothing him until he was ready to put back into his cradle. He wanted to hold him for longer, but it was not his baby and this woman was not his friend.

"He's fine," he told her when he came back to the living room.

He sat beside James Kelly, waited a while, made sure he paid the woman and they were on their way as soon as he was sure the woman was well.

On their walk to the second address, James Kelly alternated between whining for more blood and marveling quietly at the beauty of the moon. June, several times, had to steer him back in the right direction.

Their reception at the second address was much colder. The man opened the door, looked at June as though he wasn't there and scowled horribly at James Kelly.

He asked June, "You the one who set this up?"

"Sure, Junius Thompson. Kitty Parson gave me your number."

"Yeah, well, nobody mentioned anything about no niggers."

June stared and glanced at James Kelly, who didn't seem to be listening, instead fixating on a scab on the man's wrist.

"You git out, I never let no nigger chew on me, don't care for how much money," he said.

The vampire's eyes moved from the man's wrist to his face, his cheeks flushing.

"Yeah, you heard me, you bug-eyed—"

"Hey, alright, shit," June interrupted. He put his hand on the vampire's arm and turned him away. He took the list out of his pocket and scratched off the name. "Uh, I'm sorry about that, I guess...I don't know, I should have been more careful."

The vampire had started to wring his hands. "I should go back and drink him until he's dry."

"I can't let you," June said, "And it doesn't have anything to do with him. You can't keep killing people."

James Kelly had stopped walking and June turned to go back for him.

"Come on," he said. "Whatever you're feeling, talk it out with me. No more of this."

"Why not!"

"Because you don't like killing people," he said firmly. He reached out and took James Kelly by the forearm, pulling gently. "Come on, let's get out of here, go get some coffee or something."

"I need more."

"There isn't more tonight, that was our last stop," he said, "You can't skip around on the circuit. You follow it."

"We could go back to—"

"No," June said. "Come with me."

"I need—"

June took both of the vampire's hands in his and said, "I can see you're upset, but please listen to me. You cannot go back for him. Getting something else in your stomach will even you out and if it doesn't, we'll find you somewhere to feed, but leave this building with me."

James Kelly hesitated for a long time but finally let June walk him out of the building. He pulled his hands back before they left the hallway.

June brought him to a diner he knew and order coffee for both of them. June got a piece of pumpkin pie and encouraged James Kelly to eat something too.

"It'll distract you. What do you miss most?"

He looked up at the waitress, a black woman in her thirties who didn't seem to notice that June had fangs and horns. "Have you got blueberry pie?" James Kelly asked.

"It's not the season for blueberries, sorry," the waitress said.

"Try the pumpkin, it's good," June suggested. "I always get it."

"It's true, whenever we've got it," she said.

"Alright, fine," James Kelly said. He began to shred the napkin.

June reached out to touch his hand and he yanked his back. "Sorry," June said. "It's only that you look awful agitated."

"You haven't got to put your hands on me," he hissed.

"Look, now, you can't go thinking everything I do has got something to do with me liking mmm..." He glanced around the diner. "You know, who I do." He had lowered his voice, which sent an uncomfortable wave of shame through his belly. "I told you I wouldn't do anything. I wanted to help you settle a little and I know what makes me feel better."

"I...I don't mean—"

"You don't mean offense, but you know, sometimes you give it anyways."

The waitress returned with coffee and pie, setting a mug and plate before each of them. "Anything else for you two?"

"We're okay right now," June said after James Kelly said nothing.

"Alright, let me know if you need anything," she said.

The vampire sipped his coffee black while June mixed his the way he liked it. The vampire took a few bites, but mostly mangled the slice on his plate, cutting it up and mushing it around.

"You don't like it?" June asked.

"No, I...I'm thinking of other things."

"Blood still?"

He nodded.

"Try actually eating it. I hear it really does help."

James Kelly sipped his coffee and lifted another bite of pie to his mouth.

As June watched him eat and drink, restless the whole time, and wondered if he really would need to find him someone else to drink from. He thought of the reverent, fevered way he clung to people as he fed and had a terrible idea.

He had never shared his blood with a vampire before, but he knew others of his kind who had. A swallow of blood like his would set James Kelly straight for days, maybe weeks. It was powerful stuff, it would give him that slaked, full feeling that he craved.

But it wouldn't be right to offer him one addiction to replace another. And it would be selfish because he found himself wanting the vampire's mouth on him; it would be a very bad, greedy thing to feign altruism to get him to do something he didn't want to do. James Kelly had made his disinterest in men clear enough.

"You're always staring," James Kelly accused.

"I'm thinking."

"About what?"

"Lots of things. I always have questions. Curious. That's what he always said about me."

"Who?"

"My king," June said and smiled at the thought of him.

"You and him...you have some kind of thing going on?"

"No...not in the way you're thinking of." He sighed. "Anyways. You look calmer."

"I feel a little better, yes."

He waved the waitress over and got them both more coffee.

"So you didn't come right back, after the war?"

"No."

"What kind of places did she take you to?"

"All kinds of places."

"Did you make it to Italy?"

"No...we stayed mostly around Poland. Germany, Hungary. Made it to Denmark..." he said. "Norway. Northern France."

"Oh."

"It was good to come home, though. I missed New York."

"It's funny. I lived most of my life without this city ever existing, but now I don't know if I could live anywhere else."

"How long have you lived here?"

"Oh...I want to say aught three or four. He called the five of us up, asked us to keep an ear to the ground. Especially here, a lot of creatures end up in a great big place like this. We keep things settled as best we can."

James Kelly nodded.

"Uh. Speaking of which, I do sometimes go around for business. You should give me a number I can ring you at in case I'm going to be away."

"I don't know," he said, cagey and clearly having the idea that June was after him for something that would be more than friendly.

June rolled his eyes, then fixed them on James Kelly. They were nice eyes, sea glass green, and they locked eyes for a moment. Two sets of pretty eyes gazing into each other and June thought that, in a perfect world, they would lean across the table and kiss, knocking aside mugs and forks to do it.

It didn't happen. James Kelly looked away.

"Listen, kid, I can say it plain if you like," June said and, in a low voice, continued, "You're a handsome fellow and I wouldn't turn you away if you wanted me. But you don't. You made it clear and if you remind me again, I'm gonna have to ask you to find someone else to help you on this venture of yours. I can't do with this constant...distrust. Suspicion."

The vampire looked embarrassed.

"Are you at least in the phonebook?"

"No, I'll give you a phone number." He took a pen from his jacket and scribbled some digits down on a napkin, waited a moment, then added a street address. "I figure, just in case I ever don't show up, I'd like you to, if you don't mind that is, come make sure that I'm not...up to what I was before."

June took the napkin and tucked it carefully into his pocket. At home, he would copy it over into his address book.

They didn't speak much after that. They paid their bill and left a tip. June bid goodbye to the waitress, calling her by name and saying he'd be back.

They walked home and came to a point where if they went farther in the same direction, one of them would be walking the other home. They paused and looked at each other.

June felt like he had to say something, but he didn't. He took several steps away, then turned back and said, "You know what?"

James Kelly paused and glanced back at him. "Beg your pardon?"

"You got me feeling like I ought to apologize to you. You came to me asking for help and since then you've been treating me like some kind of predator. I never did a thing to you," he said.

The vampire looked at the ground.

"I didn't, did I?" June asked, hating the way his stomach had inched up into his throat.

"No."

"Cause, you know, being around you has got me feeling like I don't like who I am," he said. "And I really don't like that feeling. Is that a feeling you're at all familiar with?"

James Kelly looked up at him, then away. "It is."

"Will you stop, then?"

"June, I'm sorry. I really am," he said. "My head hasn't been on right."

June nodded but didn't feel any better.

James Kelly reached out and patted him once on the arm. "I'll see you around."

June nodded again.

They parted ways not long after that and June, once home, found that he wasn't looking forward to their next meeting.

MARCH 3, 1953

"I'M IMPRESSED, you know," June said to James Kelly as they descended from the eighth floor. It was their second stop of the night.

James Kelly looked up at him. His eyes were a little glassy. "What?"

"You let go," he said. June had still needed to call time for him, but he had released the man he'd been feeding on without needing to have hands put on him. "Now all you have to do is work on keeping time."

"Suppose so."

"So anyways. I got you something."

"What?"

"I was making eggs the other day and I forgot to set my timer, it's this little chicken shaped thing. Anyways, I forgot to set it and my egg came out hard boiled instead. Which isn't so bad."

James Kelly stared at him.

He reached into his pocket and pulled out a small silver sphere on a chain. "It's a timer. Sixty seconds exactly." He held it out.

James Kelly shook his head, slowly. "I can't..."

"Take it. You need it and I got it for free off a client."

"A client?" he asked, coming out of his daze a little.

"Sure, everybody's got to pay rent."

"What do you do for work?"

"What I'm supposed to do," he said. "People used to pray for me to come help, now they ring me up or write a letter and shell out fifty or sixty dollars."

"Pray to you?"

"Sure. I mean, who do you think worked things out Rebekah and Elizabeth and Rachel and all those other ladies from the book?"

"I don't know."

"Well, it was me. I was an angel. Say, are you going to take this thing or not, cause I got it from a clockmaker whose wife kept losing babies and I could have got a new watch instead."

James Kelly sighed and held out his hand.

June twisted the sphere, one hemisphere rotating. It clicked quietly and June placed it in the vampire's hand.

They continued on their way out the building and once a minute had ticked by, the timer dinged, startling James Kelly.

June smiled at that and said, "You didn't say thank you."

The vampire turned a little pink around the cheeks. "Thank you."

"You're welcome. I'm just teasing, though. You ready for spring?"

"I imagine I don't have a choice either way."

"No, none of us do."

James Kelly said, "Baseball season, though, that will be good."

June glanced at him, not knowing what to say. He didn't know much about baseball; human sports had never interested him. "I have another stop to make, a few blocks over."

"Oh."

"You can come if you'd like. Or head home. But I've got to turn up there."

"What kind of stop?"

"For work. Checking in on someone. New parents, you know how they worry."

"I suppose I could," James Kelly said, which took June by surprise. He normally declined invitations to accompany June anywhere but to get blood or coffee, and the coffee usually required persistence.

James Kelly followed him down the street when he turned and said after a while, "I don't know if this is a great place for me to be. I ought to head back, I think."

June glanced at him and looked ahead. He saw a pair of police officers and understood his concern immediately; they had come to an affluent white neighborhood after all. He squinted at the officers and said, "That's just Tom and Bernie, though, they know me."

"You're sure? It's the middle of the night."

"Don't worry, not if you're with me."

They continued their approach and June raised his hand to hail the police officers. "Hi!"

"Hey there, June," one said.

After that, no other words were exchanged and they did nothing more to James Kelly than give him a sideways look. June knocked on the door of a townhouse and was immediately let in by young, light-skinned black woman in a maid's uniform.

She let June in and glanced at James Kelly, unsure.

"Hi, Gladys. Don't worry, he's with me."

"The Bakers and the baby are upstairs," she said, quiet and unhappy.

June frowned at her. "Is something wrong?"

"You ought to go up and talk to them."

June nodded and looked at James Kelly. "Maybe you should wait here."

The vampire nodded.

June headed upstairs and found the Bakers in the same room in which he had last seen them, the only difference that Mrs. Baker was no longer heavily pregnant. She was seated upright in bed with a tray of barely touched food before her. Her husband sat in an armchair beside the bed. In the corner of the room sat a bassinet that neither parent seemed to notice.

He stepped into the room and said, "I got your call. Is everything going okay?"

"No," came the clipped, harsh answer from Mr. Baker. "You promised us a healthy baby."

His stomach started to knot and June asked, "What's the problem?"

"It's...a monster," the man said.

June looked to the mother.

"Look at it yourself," she said.

He went over and peered into the bassinet and saw a normal looking child, not more than a day old. The baby looked and smelled perfectly normal to him, no hint of sickness; it was nothing more than fussy and hungry. He glanced back at the parents and said, "I don't see anything wrong."

"Uncover it."

He pulled a blanket off the child and before anything else, was appalled to see that it had on no diaper or clothes beneath the blanket that had been tossed over it.

"You said the child would be healthy," the mother accused. "Not deformed."

"Some kind of...hermaphrodite," the father hissed. "Fit for a freak show. I should have known something bad would come from making a deal with a demon."

He looked back at the baby and performed a closer inspection, seeing that it had male and female parts between the legs. He sighed. "There's nothing to be done about that."

The parents stared at him.

He looked around the room and saw all the clothes and supplies that had been gathered for the care of the child. They had been jubilant as expectant parents, well supplied and over prepared. That had all fallen aside, clearly.

Before he could bring himself to speak to them again, he lifted the child to his chest to cradle it. "Let's get you taken care of." He diapered and dressed the baby and kept it in his arms, feeling calmer with a tiny life held close. "Are you going to feed her?" he asked the mother.

"Her?" the father demanded.

The mother answered, "I fed it for as long as I could bear."

"Babies need to eat," he insisted. "What's your plan for this child?"

"You can't fix it?" the mother asked softly.

"There's nothing that needs to be fixed," he said firmly. "You've got a little girl and she's kind of different, sure, but it's not something to be fixed."

"How can you say that's a girl?"

"Because she is," he said. "It's just something I can...feel. It comes with the territory, so take my word on it."

"It has a penis," the father hissed.

"You say that like there aren't other girls like that," June said. "What is your plan for this child?" he asked again.

"You promise that it's a girl?" the mother asked.

"Right now and as far as I can tell, you have a daughter. I recall you wanted to name her Olivia."

The baby began to fuss again, very hungry and tired. June looked at the mother, not sure what else he could do to convince her.

"Mister, I went out and bought some of that evaporated milk," a sad voice from the doorway told him. "And bottles."

June glanced over to see two brown faces, James Kelly and the maid. He looked to the parents once more and then nodded at the maid. He followed her down to the kitchen and rocked the baby while they waited. She calmed a little and Gladys offered to take her when the bottle was ready, but June shook his head and took the bottle instead.

He sat, holding the baby tighter than really necessary, but he had started to shake all over and feared that he might drop her, even though he had only dropped a baby once in all his thousands of years. He spoke softly with her while he fed her, making sure she knew her name and that she was lovely.

"The doctor, he came by for the birth, you know," Gladys said as she watched him, "He said that they could do surgery to have...you know, have it removed, but Mr. and Mrs. Baker thought you could fix it easier."

He glanced up at her.

"I'm glad they called you," she said.

"Me too."

James Kelly watched silently, leaning against the kitchen counter with his hands in his pockets.

"You mean it when you say she's a girl?"

June nodded. He set the emptied bottle aside and patted the baby's back.

"You should have heard Mr. Baker raging. I was afraid he'd do something...drastic," she said.

"I don't want to hear that," June said.

Something clattered and they looked over to see that James Kelly had elbowed the drying rack and knocked a pan into the sink. He hurried to pick it up and return it. June smiled a little bit.

With flushed cheeks, James Kelly said, "What are we doing here anyways? I'm sure Annie's wondering where I've gotten to."

"You can go."

"I don't...I wouldn't want to be out alone at this time of night," he said.

June considered him for a moment. "What are you worried about, anyways? If anyone gave you a hard time, you could set them straight."

James Kelly shook his head. "Not without doing something I don't want to. And I was never one for fighting."

Olivia burped and June wiped spit-up from her face. "What are we going to do with you, anyways? And what about your mother and father?"

"If she stays...if they keep her," Gladys said, "My brother works here, too, we'd keep a good eye on her. Rich folk have the maids raise their babies anyways."

"And you'd be sure to give me a call if anything were to happen?" June asked. "Of any sort."

She nodded.

"It's certainly not ideal..." June said. He adjusted the child in his arms and headed back upstairs. He went directly over to Mrs. Baker and pushed the baby into her arms. She flinched a little, but he didn't know if that was because of Olivia or him. Some people had a hard time seeing past his fangs, horns, and claws.

"This is your daughter, her name is Olivia," he said, stepping back when he was sure she had a grip on the baby. "Look at her and tell me right now if you're going to turn her out because I can find a real home for her if you won't give her one."

"I don't like the tone you're taking," Mr. Baker warned.

June turned to look at him for just a moment, his eyes as cold as he could make him, then looked back to Mrs. Baker. To both of them, he said, "And if you keep her and I find that you've ever done a thing to harm her, so help me, I'll get every monster out of hell up in Manhattan to deal with you."

They stared.

"And considering the trouble you had making her, this is the last chance you get for a baby because there's no way I'd help you make another one," he warned.

Husband and wife looked at each other.

"Kevin, he says she's healthy..." Mrs. Baker said.

Mr. Baker still looked uncertain and angry.

June glanced at the way Mrs. Baker had adjusted herself to hold Olivia. "Have you held her yet?" he asked the man.

He shook his head minimally, lips tight together.

"Give her a hold, come on," June said, taking the baby and bringing her over to her father, who still sat rigidly in his armchair. He took the baby when June handed her to him, but the way he might have taken a bundle of dirty laundry. "Dad, come on, look at that face and tell me you're not sold!" June prompted with a smile.

Mr. Baker looked down at the baby and made a scrunched, uncomfortable face that made June question the decision to have him hold her. He started to cough, or maybe choke, and June looked at Mrs. Baker, but before she could say anything the man started to rasp apologies at the baby.

"I think you can go," Mrs. Baker said.

"Keep my number, just in case," June said and backed out of the room.

He went to the kitchen, made Gladys promise to keep an eye on things and headed for the door.

James Kelly followed him out the door and asked, "Is that normal?"

"Well, the whole night was sort of odd, so which particular part are you talking about?" June said.

"I don't know," James Kelly said. "You don't figure people would want to get rid of their babies."

June laughed. "People have been throwing away babies since they've been having them. I mean, if you don't *want* a child, that's one thing and you can make arrangements, of course, but all these people wanting this...perfect little idealized thing that doesn't cry or fuss or look a little funny. I had a woman once call me because her six-year-old went deaf after the measles. That's got nothing to do with me! Or if a baby's born with an extra toe or two. That's got nothing to do with healthy!" He paused for a moment and saw that the vampire was staring at him. "What?"

James Kelly shrugged. "You're more worked up about this than you were about me showing up to your house all addled and bloody."

"Yes, well, babies are my business. Bad crop rotation bugs the hell out of me, too," he said. "In a different way, I suppose."

James Kelly smiled at him and they walked together until they had to part ways.

JUNE AND James Kelly sat in the diner, each with coffee in front of them. June finished his last sip and asked, "Say, you're from Brooklyn, right?" even though he knew the answer.

James Kelly nodded.

"You like the Dodgers?"

"Sure I do!" James Kelly said.

June reached into his jacket and pulled out a pair of tickets. "I'm not really one for sports and I helped out one of the players get a family underway." He slid the tickets across the table.

James Kelly took them up. "These are for the first game of the season!"

"Sure," June said. "Anyways, I figure you can take your girl."

"Annie doesn't like baseball. Or any sport. Says they're for peasants. And she still won't go out in the sun."

June snorted. "Well, find a friend, then," he said.

"You really don't want these?" the vampire asked.

"No. I'm like your girl, I don't care for sports."

"Come with me," James Kelly said. "I mean, these are good seats, if anything will turn you on to the game, seats on the first baseline will. *Everybody* likes baseball."

"Except for your girl."

"She's been dead for two hundred years," James Kelly said and shrugged.

"And she won't be sore? I get the feeling she's not keen on me, judging how she answered the phone yesterday."

"She's just stubborn."

June looked at the date on the tickets. April fourteenth. He had called James Kelly the other day to let him know that he was going away for four days and James Kelly had assured him that he would be able to do his circuit on his own. April fourteenth would be the day after he got back and it would give him the chance to check on James Kelly after nearly a week without supervision.

One more day of not keeping an eye on him might not do any harm, but it could also do an awful lot of harm.

"Sure, I'll give it a go," June said, "Can't spent all of the vastness of time never trying anything new." He smiled broadly at James Kelly.

The vampire smiled back.

They paid their bill and left a tip. On their walk home, June paused on the street where they normally parted ways. "You're sure you'll be able to do it on your own?"

"I'll be fine," James Kelly assured.

June patted his shoulder and gave a gentle squeeze. "I think you will be."

James Kelly pulled himself out of June's grip, his face carefully arranged not to show discomfort. June had almost gotten used to that face.

"Did your parents not hug you or something?" June asked, trying to joke.

"My parents were fine," he said.

"It bothers you, though," June said, "I'm sorry."

James Kelly shrugged. "I'll come by before the game."

June nodded, feeling much better at that gentle reminder that their plans would remain the same.

The next morning, June left on a circuit of the state, visiting several dozen families and farms from the sound up to the border. Every so many months, once he had enough work to make the trip worth his time, he went around and helped the people he could with their fertility woes. Since the war had ended, June had found his services very much in demand and he liked that fine.

He thought a few times about calling into the check on the vampire but didn't. The night he got back, he dropped a line and Anastasia answered, not at all happy to be hearing from him.

"Hi, is James Kelly around?"

"Yes."

"You figure I can talk to him?"

"I will see if he will take your call."

June waited by the phone for several minutes, wondering what could be taking so long. After nearly five minutes ticked past, someone picked up the phone and a ragged voice answered, "Hello?"

"Hi, I figured I should let you know that I'm back in town, make sure we're still on for tomorrow."

A long moment passed before the vampire answered, "Yes. Sorry, it almost slipped my mind."

"You alright? You sound...kind of sick."

"I...uh. The circuit...I couldn't do it alone."

"You didn't!" June cried. "Killing one of them gets important people upset! Things above my head, I don't have a lot of pull with the vamp gangs."

"No, I didn't go. I couldn't," James Kelly said.

June hated to hear the shake in his tone. In the background, he heard Anastasia telling him that this nonsense was out of control, that he was making himself sick. He thought that James Kelly must have turned his head away from the phone because what he shouted back to her came through the phone muffled.

"Sorry," the vampire said.

June heard Anastasia telling James Kelly that she wouldn't have chosen him if she'd know he'd be so weak.

"Listen, why don't you pack a change of clothes...you know, I'll see if some of the people you skipped will take you tonight, and you can crash here," he said. "If things are tense," he added because he didn't want to presume.

"I think...maybe that would be a good idea..."

"See you soon." He hung up and dialed people on the circuit until he got two yeses. He went outside to smoke and wait for James Kelly, who arrived looking like absolute shit. June stubbed out his cigarette and said, "What in the world *happened* to you?"

"I just need to drink something."

June squinted at him. "You've already been drinking something."

"Coffee takes the edge off, I thought something stronger might work better."

"Oh, you poor simple thing," June said and took the bag he had packed. He lit James Kelly a cigarette and ran his bag upstairs. "Ready?" he asked when he returned.

The vampire nodded.

"Hooch doesn't work the way coffee or food can," June said. "Smoking takes the edge off, too."

James Kelly nodded. He continued to smoke and smoked for the whole walk to their first stop.

June brought him to the first place and then the second, keeping a careful eye on him and pulling him back from the people from whom he drank. After so many days, June wasn't surprised he wasn't fully in control.

As they walked out from the second apartment building, June glanced at James Kelly and said, "Oh, come here. You'll get people worrying."

James Kelly, in his usual post-feeding tranquility, did not pull away when June wiped a smear of blood from his face. He even rested his cheek against June's hand for a few moments. It meant nothing, June told himself; some vampires got this way after they fed, craving closeness and skin contact.

"Let's get you home, you can cuddle with Gordon," June said.

James Kelly pulled back. "I don't have any interest in anyone named *Gordon*."

"Gordon is the cat," June said.

He looked a little ashamed, but blood and the alcohol before had loosened his tongue so he said, "Nothing against you, but I just don't have any interest in that unnatural stuff. It's not...it's not the way things are supposed to be."

June considered letting it go and when he looked into the vampire's addled face, he knew anything he said would be pointless. Instead, he put his hand on James Kelly's arm and directed him towards home.

The vampire leaned against him, seemingly unaware of what he had said before. June made him coffee and got him settled in on the couch.

June sat on the coffee table and sipped his own drink.

After he'd finished the coffee, James Kelly looked at him and said, "I shouldn't have said that."

"You bring it up more than I do," June said. "It makes me think you've got something on your mind." He tried to keep his voice as mild as he could, without a hint of accusation.

"No," he said harshly and then looked reticent.

"You were born. Mom and Dad got together and threw what they had together," he said, "And they didn't know what they would get. No control. But you know, I wasn't born."

James Kelly looked at him.

"I was made. Do you know who made me?"

"The Devil?"

June laughed. "No. God. God made me. He made all the angels. I was an angel, don't forget. God made me, exactly the way I am. Sure, the body is sort of a new deal, but you get used to it after a few hundred lifetimes. So you can't tell me that I'm not the way I'm supposed to be. You're a collection of happenstance, generations of people rolling the dice and not knowing what they'll get. But I was made and I was made just the way He wanted."

James Kelly looked down at his mug.

"And anyways as far as bodies go, I like this one. I like the colors."

The vampire didn't look up.

"Do you want another cup of coffee?"

"Please."

June reached out and took the mug. When he returned, James Kelly asked, "You were really an angel?"

"I can't prove it, so you'll just have to take my word," he said.

"But if you were an angel...I mean, what it says..."

"None of those holy books popped down from heaven, you know," he said with a shrug. They didn't talk much as they drank their second cup. Coffee before bed might not have been a great way to get to sleep, but it helped the vampire keep his thirst under control.

"You feeling better?" June asked.

James Kelly nodded.

June looked over at the window and saw the cat on the fire escape. He went over and let him in. The cat brushed against his hand and June picked him up. He brought the cat over to James Kelly and said, "This is Gordon."

James Kelly nodded.

"He's very friendly," June said. "Sometimes...you know how cats are."

The cat jumped from his arms to the couch, where he settled on one of the arms. He eyed the vampire warily, his little black nose sniffing.

"I'm going to bed. We've got stuff to do in the morning. If you still want to go to the game."

"Of course."

June stood up and headed for the kitchen and deposited their mugs in the sink. He would deal with them at some other point; being a bachelor meant no one could tell him not to leave things where he wanted to leave them.

On his way back through the living room, he saw that James Kelly had not settled into the couch. "Did you bring pajamas?" he asked, wondering if that was what had stalled him.

"Yes."

"Oh. Just making sure. You look uncomfortable."

"I'm sort of worried."

June glanced towards his bedroom door and then returned to his seat on the coffee table. "Worried about what? Not about this blood thing? You're doing much better than you were."

"No, it's not about that."

"Want to share?"

"I assume that in your many years, you've had relationships."

"Yes."

"I'm not sure what to do about Annie. She's...unhappy that I'm doing this."

"That you don't want to kill people anymore?"

"I *never* wanted to kill people," James Kelly said.

June made a face. "I don't know."

"Don't give me that!"

"I think you're holding back, James Kelly, I really do. I don't know if it's out of love for your woman or because you like that rush of taking a life...but she encourages you to kill and you've stayed with her."

"Because I want to help her!"

"Alright, settle yourself," June soothed. "You're the worried one."

James Kelly looked at his hands. "I don't know what to do."

"Talk to her. Really sit down and talk to her, none of that back and forth bickering. Talking is always the right thing to do," he said.

"I tried. In a way."

"Tell her it's important to you, make sure she knows," June said. "And if she won't listen, maybe you ought to think about moving on."

"I couldn't."

"You don't want to," June said, "I'm not blaming you, it's hard to end something like that. But you have to think about what's right for both of you."

In a quiet voice that made him seem vulnerable, James Kelly

asked, "Have you ended a lot of relationships?"

June rubbed the back of his neck. "It's been a long time since I've had a relationship to end. I mean, there's been *people*, these here and there, come and go things that peter out on their own."

"Oh."

"It's been a long time since things have felt...I don't know what the right word is. Homey? Comfortable? With someone," he said. "You know, that feeling that you can wake up next to someone every morning and always want them to be there."

James Kelly nodded.

"Anyways, we're not talking about me," June said. "You should try to sleep."

The vampire nodded again.

June headed towards bed and from behind him he heard, "Thanks for talking."

"Anytime."

APRIL 14, 1953

AS THEY walked home after a Dodgers win and two successful feeding sessions where James Kelly had set his timer and pulled himself back as soon as it dinged, June looked up at the sky and wondered where all the stars had gone. He remembered, in a painful flash, the stars on the first night he had spent on earth after being cast out.

He looked at the vampire who walked on clouds beside him. He had been dreamily recounting parts of the game for June, asking him half a dozen times if he had changed his mind about baseball.

"I mean, you have to at least admit it's a good sport, even if you don't like it," the vampire insisted.

"I said I liked it fine," he said, smiling at the other man more fondly than he should have.

"Quit looking at me like that."

June pressed his lips together and felt his face grow warm. "Like what?" he asked, his words clipped.

"Like I'm stupid."

"Well, sure, but stupid like a puppy, not in a bad way," June said, the tight feeling in his chest evaporating.

"It's just...the sound of the bat when there's a good solid hit? You can't compare!"

"Alright, if I say I'm sold, will you *stop?*" June asked.

James Kelly smiled. "It's been a while since I've been to a

game."

"If you don't go out in the day and you don't go to games, what is it that you and your girl do together?"

"Annie likes Fifth Avenue. She likes Central Park, likes to walk around at night and see who else is out at night. We go down to the Battery and listen to the harbor noises."

"Oh."

"She likes to play records; we listen to a lot of records. And she reads to me."

"She reads to you?"

James Kelly nodded and shrugged. "I don't know, it makes her happy and it doesn't bother me." He went quiet for a moment, then, with a nervous glance at the creature who walked beside him, said, "The first fellow she turned...he couldn't read. She would read to him. I think she misses him..."

"Do you know what happened to him?"

"They had some kind of falling out. She won't tell me the details. I...I don't know. Never mind."

"You can tell me," June encouraged gently.

"Sometimes I think I might be a replacement."

June didn't know what to say to that, but he badly wanted to say something because the vampire sounded so forlorn. He reached out to touch James Kelly but pulled his hand back. James Kelly watched him do it and his golden brown eyes followed June's hand as it moved back to his side.

"Sorry," June said, "That you feel that way. I think you need to have a real talk with her."

James Kelly glanced around and asked, "Are you following me home?"

June looked too. He had walked past the street where they usually split up. "Oh. Figure I am at this point. I was too busy getting convinced that baseball is the world's greatest sport."

The vampire stared at him for a moment.

"I can head back."

"No, you know, maybe you can...I don't know. You've been helping me a lot, maybe Annie will take your word on this better than mine. You're older than both of us."

"You want me to talk to her for you?"

He nodded, not able to look June in the eyes.

"I'll give it a shot."

"Thanks."

They walked for a few more blocks until James Kelly stopped in front of an apartment building. They both remained silent as James Kelly unlocked the door and they walked up six flights of stairs. The vampire hesitated before the door to his apartment, then sighed and opened the door. There was music playing and June wanted to say it was one of Chopin's nocturnes, but he could have been wrong.

James Kelly entered and gestured for June to follow him. He called, "Annie?"

"In the living room."

"I, uh, I brought someone with me," he said, closing the door behind him.

Anastasia appeared a moment later, in a slip and silk robe, her red-blonde hair tumbling over her shoulders. Before she looked at June, she said, "I knew you would give up on this nonsense." She took the other vampire's face in her hands and kissed him. "I knew you would see."

"Annie," he said, taking her hands. "I haven't changed my mind."

She looked at June and then pulled her hands back. She made a sound of disgust and walked away into the living room, folding her robe around herself.

James Kelly followed after her and June followed him.

"Annie, I know you think I'm being foolish—"

"What are you thinking, bringing some other man here?" she demanded. "I'm not dressed. It's not decent."

"I can wait until you're dressed if you want," June offered.

"You don't have to wait for anything, you can go, I do not want to talk to you," she said.

"Annie, please," James Kelly said. "This is important to me. June, please, come in and have a seat."

June sat on the couch.

Anastasia fixed her eyes on him and said, "Well, what is it? What nonsense are you twisting up in his head so that he spends nights away from home?"

"He came to me, you know, and I'm trying to help him do what he wants," June said. "He's doing very well and he's put a lot of work in."

"You are trying to tell him that vampires do not need to kill."

"You don't. I can't name four or five *dozen* off the top of my head who live without killing, and some who have never taken a life."

"It is not natural."

June sighed then said, "I am much older than you and vampires don't need to kill any more than humans need to smoke opium. It's something that feels good. The need for blood is not something I'm denying, but there are safe ways to get what you need."

She bared her teeth and he was tempted to bare his.

"Even if it's not what you want, you shouldn't push what you want on him."

"I *made* him, *I* am vampire, you cannot understand," she said. She turned towards James Kelly and asked, "Don't you see that he cannot understand you? You are not the same. There is no way."

"I don't like hurting people, Annie, I hate it," he said and June thought he heard James Kelly's voice waver.

"Shh, no," she said, "See what he has done? You were happy. So excited to come home." She took his face in her hands again.

"I need you to support me in this, Annie, if I can't keep hurting people, I can't do it," he said. He wrapped his arms around her and buried his face in her shoulder. "Please. I need you."

"And you have me," she said, returning the embrace. "Tell your friend to go and we will talk."

She kissed him tenderly and June examined his claws for a moment until James Kelly looked at him and opened his mouth, but June cut him off, saying, "I'll see myself out. Don't forget we have business tomorrow."

James Kelly nodded.

June let himself out and took a long walk home. He stayed out on the stoop and smoked for about an hour until he was ready to go inside.

Once inside, he looked at the phone, hesitated, then picked it up, dialing a number he hadn't in months.

"Lo?" came the answer after half a dozen rings.

"You still wake?"

"June?"

"Aye. Did I wake you?"

"No. D'ya need somefin?"

"You want to come over?"

"Don' see why not. See you in a bit."

"Thanks."

They both hung up and twenty minutes later, a small surge of panic rushed through him when he heard the door open. He put his hand over his heart and said, "Forgot I gave you a key."

The other man closed the door behind him and gave him a smile, his fangs showing just a little. He had pale golden skin, one arm and red eyes, eyes that marked him as one of the Devil's descendants. Across his face ran a large scar that clouded one of his eyes and tugged at his mouth on one side. He'd been born without the arm and he'd gotten the scar in a gang turf war.

Wei had been born in the eighteen-thirties in China but had grown up in London. At the age of eight, he'd lost his mother and had been taken in by one of the gangs of creatures in the city.

"How you been?" Wei asked.

June shrugged.

"Y'look sad," he said, putting aside his jacket and coming over to June's side, putting a hand on his arm.

June folded against him immediately.

"Oi, watch them horns, you'll put m'other eye out," Wei warned.

"Sorry," June murmured.

Wei kissed his hair and, keeping his arm around June, walked over to the couch. "Tell me what y'need."

"I want to go home," June said.

"Oh, you pathetic man," Wei said.

June sighed.

They settled onto the couch together and June curled him against the other man. "I just need to be held for a little while..."

"Course."

A FEW nights later, June waited, smoking, on the stoop for the vampire and when he saw James Kelly, he asked, "You work things out with your girl?"

"We talked it out for a while," James Kelly said. He glanced at Wei.

"He's a friend, don't worry, he's not tagging along. No need to get nervous."

"A friend?"

"Sure, waters my plants and keeps an eye on Gordon when I'm out of town," June said.

"Are you going out of town?" the vampire asked, an edge of fear creeping into his voice.

June smiled. "No."

James Kelly glanced between them again.

"Ready to go?" June asked.

The vampire nodded.

Wei reached out and put a hand on June's shoulder, giving it a squeeze. "See you soon." He swooped down and kissed June's cheek, then turned to go inside.

June stood and began to walk. The vampire followed behind him.

"You can say it, whatever you're thinking," June said.

"Is that one of the come and go, here and there things you were talking about?" James Kelly asked.

"That's Wei," June said. "He's a friend, like I said, no need to call it more than that."

"Oh."

"I've just been a little bit homesick and it helps to have a friend around."

"When you say homesick...?"

"For heaven."

"If you wanted to be in heaven, why did you—"

"That is a long answer, I don't want to get into it right now," June said. "Ask me again some other time."

James Kelly nodded.

They walked in silence after that. June watched on as James Kelly fed. They didn't say much on their way to their second visit either. Outside the door of the apartment, June stopped and said, "You go in on your own."

"What?"

"I think you can do it. I really do. Give it a go."

"June..."

June reached out and put both hands on the vampire's shoulders. "Listen, you can do this, all on your own."

"What if I can't?"

"Do you worry about everything this much?"

"Just about killing people!"

"Oh, shhh, no shouting," he said. He turned the vampire so he faced towards the door. "Go on."

His hands, brown and soft looking, trembled when he reached out to knock on the door. The tenant answered and let him in. He entered, with one glance back at June.

June waited outside the door, unconcerned and leaning against the wall. Several people passed him and gave him strange looks; one little boy waved to him and he waved back. No more than five minutes went by before James Kelly reemerged.

"Did you rend any throats?" June asked.

James Kelly shook his head.

"Coffee?"

He shook his head again. "No, thank you. Annie and I have plans for the early morning."

"Oh, sounds fun," he said and followed after him as they left the building. "So...do you think that you need me coming with you for these things anymore?"

James Kelly stopped walking and June bumped into him. "What do you mean?"

"I mean, do you really need me watching you while you feed?" he asked.

"You...if you don't want to come. I can...I just worry."

"I'm not saying I won't come," June amended. "If you want support, I'll give it to you, but..." He rubbed the back of his neck, thinking of the fevered, desperate way that the vampire pressed his mouth against the people he fed from, trying not to let his mind wander to the things it reminded him of. "I think you can do it on your own."

"I don't know."

"Think on it."

The vampire nodded. "I'll give it a try, I guess."

Neither said much until they bid farewell as they parted ways. June did not like that it had been such a quiet night between them. He wished they could have gotten coffee again.

Inside his apartment, he found Wei and Gordon on the couch.

"Didja do it?" Wei asked.

June nodded.

"Oh, poor fing, you look so sad." He held out his hand and June took it. He curled up on his lap and Wei said, "Wif your *horns*, June, be careful!"

"Sorry."

Gordon leaped away from them with a disdainful meow.

"You need t'find someone, June."

"I can't, everyone I like is taken or straight or *both* or they don't like me," he said.

"You need t'find somefin, then, somefin to make this place into a home," Wei said. He ran his fingers over one of June's horns. "What were you like before?"

"Before what?" June asked, pretending he didn't know what he meant.

"Before Georgia."

"I don't want to talk about Georgia or before Georgia or anything about any of that," he said.

Wei didn't say anything and June couldn't think of anything to add. He reached up and wrapped his fingers around Wei's hands.

"Thank you," June said.

"Friends are for helping."

"You want to help me get laid?"

Wei didn't laugh, even though June knew his tone had been perfectly teasing. Instead, he said, "I can arrange something if you'd like. You know, I thought the market for male companionship would dwindle when the war was over, but you'd be surprised who comes asking around now."

"Hmm?"

"Soldiers comin home wif funny ideas in their heads, you know, or funny sorts of memories of what they did wif no women around…"

"Mmm," June hummed, not sure what else to say.

"Soldiers like that friend of yours," Wei said mildly.

June snorted. "I told you, you're being ridiculous. He jumps to high heaven when I give him a pat on the arm."

"And I seen men beggin to get sucked off one minute and threatenin beat the shit out of the fellow for doin it the next," Wei said.

"I don't want to talk about James Kelly, anyways. Who've you got to set me up with?"

"Mmm, I fink you'd like Micah. Or Finnian."

"Micah?"

"Lots of freckles."

June sighed.

"All over," Wei added.

June licked his lips. "Alright."

"You'll feel better."

With a snort, June said, "Course I will."

"No more thinking about vampires with those pretty curls—"

"Cut it out!" June said. "I'm hungry, do you want to go out?"

"Sure, but what's open?"

"I know a place, don't worry."

They went out for something to eat, sharing the diner with the other late night good-for-nothings.

WEI WENT home in the morning and before the week was out, he sent Micah to visit June, with the warning to treat him very nicely. June let him in and looked him over; he had not expected a human and this young man had clearly not expected something blue with horns and claws to be his client.

Of course, Wei had not thought to warn him, he'd grown up surrounded by creatures, and June felt terrible seeing the quick, nervous darting of his brown eyes as he glanced around June's apartment.

"Can I get you something?" June asked.

"No, I'm fine."

"You sure? I can make some coffee or something." He did not remember when this compulsion to offer coffee to everyone who set foot in his apartment had started, but it was a habit he couldn't shake.

Micah shook his head again.

"Come on, kid, you're killing me," June said, "You look so scared."

A blush came to the human's pale cheeks. "I've never...you know, you look *different*. I didn't expect..."

June chewed on one of his claws, a nervous habit that everyone chastised him for. "Do you want to go?"

"No, you're a friend of Wei's."

June sighed. "Well, come in past the door," he said.

Micah came in a little farther, heading uncertainly towards the couch. He looked at June and then quickly away.

"What did you want to ask?" June asked.

"I'm...just wondering what you are."

"One of the fallen," he said.

"Oh. Wait, like an angel?"

He nodded.

"Have you got wings?"

"No. Don't you think you'd have noticed?"

Micah turned pink again. "Anyways, Wei says to do whatever you want for the night but, uh, if it's all the same to you, I don't care for rough stuff."

"That's fine," he said. "Let me get your jacket?"

Micah nodded and June helped him slip out of his jacket and hung it up for him. When he walked back over, the human put a hand on his arm and June stopped. Micah rested his other hand on June's hip and stepped a little closer.

"So you have to tell me what you want," the young man said, close enough that they were mostly touching.

June could feel his breath on his neck; it smelled of mint. He wanted everything, the whole world, he wanted a mouth to press against him as hungrily as it pressed against the skin it drank from, but that would never happen.

"I want you to tell me stop if I do something you don't like," June said. "And I want to kiss you. Can we start with that?"

Micah nodded, so June leaned in closer and kissed first his neck and then his jaw, and then his mouth, winding an arm around him to hold him. After their kiss, he rested his head against Micah's shoulder, careful with his horns, and wondered if Wei had meant it when he'd said he had freckles all over.

He ran his fingers along the buttons on his shirt and started to undo them, revealing pale skin dotted all over with freckles. "You said for the night?"

"Yes."

"When do you have to go?"

"I have someone else to see at noon."

"Do you get tired of it?" June asked, his hands still working on Micah's clothes, untucking his shirt and unfastening his belt, "Or do you like your work?"

"It's okay, I mean...Wei keeps an eye out for us and the money's pretty good, but it's...kind of scary sometimes. Not knowing what might happen," he said. "Why?"

"I don't know, I keep feeling like I have to say something because I don't know you."

"Do you always know the people you sleep with?" he asked.

June thought about the question, then answered, "Yes." He put a hand on Micah's arm and moved him towards the couch. "Can you...you know, can we get undressed?"

Micah smiled. "It's kind of what I'm here for."

June shed some of his clothes while the human removed all of his. The demon stopped to look at the young man, feeling both desire and an odd detachment from the situation. He'd asked Wei for sex, but he began to realize that sex was not what he'd been craving, at least, not entirely. There was no denying that he wanted to be with someone, but he wanted it in a way that required caring and tenderness as well as longing.

But Micah was here and he was covered in pretty little speckles, so he would do for now. June kissed him again and Micah slipped his hands inside June's clothes. His hands were a little cold as they roamed across June's body.

The creature shed the rest of his clothing and tangled himself around the human. They started on the couch and ended in the bedroom, taking turns with each other until they were sweaty and tired.

"You can stay, right?" June asked, lying on his stomach, his face nestled against his pillow. He fought to keep his eyes open. "Until the morning, at least?"

Micah yawned and rubbed his eyes.

"Please."

"I usually don't."

June nodded.

The human yawned again. "Maybe...I don't know, just a nap, though, before I head home."

June smiled and reached out to hold him.

"And you know, guys usually don't pay so much attention to me."

"You're good-looking, why wouldn't they?" June asked.

"No, I mean that they don't care what I want."

"More fun if we're both having fun, though, isn't it?" It was the last thing he could manage. Micah might have said something else, but June didn't hear it, drifting off with his forehead against the other man's chest.

He woke in the middle of the night without knowing why. He

closed his eyes and tried to go back to sleep, but realized his phone was ringing. He rubbed his eyes and went to the living room to answer it, wondering if it was Wei or a worried client.

"June?"

"Anastasia?"

"Yes. James Kelly did not come home. He went out on that ridiculous...circuit you have him doing. He has been gone for hours."

"Oh."

"He is not with you?"

"No."

She sighed.

"Maybe he just wanted time on his own."

"Why would he want that?" she demanded and June knew that he had said the wrong thing.

"Sometimes people do, that's all," he soothed. "But he's not here. If he comes around, I'll tell him...uh." He stared out the window.

"What?"

"I'll tell him you called."

"Thank you," she said without sounding grateful at all.

He hung up and went over to the window, where Gordon sat, which was not unexpected. He went to the window to go in and out; the unusual part was that beside him on the fire escape sat a vampire who, a moment ago, had been trying to open the window.

June opened his window. "What are you doing?"

James Kelly shrugged, with the look of a kid who'd been caught doing something bad. He could not look at June. "I don't know. I was, uh, on my way home and I took a sort of detour."

"Were you trying to come in my window?"

"No, Gordon was, I heard him meowing and, you know, I thought, I can just pop up and let him in."

June frowned.

"And the window was locked and I'm not good at all with heights I'm realizing at this moment in my life."

June grinned. "Are you *stuck* on my fire escape?"

"I might be."

"Well, might as well come in, I can let you out the usual way. What were you doing taking a detour by my place?"

As he climbed in through the window, James Kelly said, "Annie and I were at it again, I didn't want to go home." Once inside, he glanced around the apartment and looked at June for the first time, then immediately looked away. "You've got someone else here."

"Sure."

He headed right for the door. "I'm sorry, I'm making a real idiot out of myself these days."

"Hey, now, wait," June said. "Tell me how you did feeding at least?"

Micah came from the bedroom, wearing nothing, a blanket half wrapped around him, clutched against his chest and not hiding anything that he might have wanted to hide. "June? Is everything alright? What time is it?"

"It's just past two, go back to sleep. The cat wanted to come in."

The human could not see in the dark the way the vampire could, so though Micah did not notice James Kelly, James Kelly noticed him, staring at him, then looking away.

"Okay," Micah said through a yawn, heading back to the bedroom, his feet shuffling against the floor.

"You alright? You look faint," June said to him once Micah had left. He had the feeling that if he put an ear to the vampire's chest, his heart would have been rushing faster than a hummingbird's wings. "What's got you worked up?" he asked, recalling the suspicions that Wei had voiced.

"I have to go," he said, struggling to open the door, fighting with the lock before he managed to open it.

"Hey!" June called after him, worried.

The vampire turned back to face him briefly and said, sounding close to tears, "I can't do this, June, I just *can't*."

He sped away after that, almost running.

June dodged back inside, grabbed a robe and went after him; it did not feel right to let him leave like that. He caught up and touched his arm, saying, "Listen, whatever you can't do, I can help you out."

He yanked his arm back. "Don't touch me."

"Sorry. You seem upset."

"No, I...I need to go home and fix things with Annie. Not this. I don't need anything else from you."

Startled by the anger in his last statement, June said, "Well...I mean. Shit. If you ever do, though, hold on to my number, okay?"

"I won't!"

"Alright, just remember, you were the one on my fire escape."

"Don't go looking into it, I've had enough of your fag bullshit."

June blinked a few times, not knowing what else he could do. He wouldn't let that hurt him; he had no business feeling hurt over that, not when he knew that he had been made exactly right, not ill-made in any aspect.

The vampire stormed off and June went back to bed, crawling in beside Micah, not knowing what he would do the next time he needed someone to lie against.

It did not hurt, he realized, to be insulted, it hurt because James Kelly had been the one to do it and June had been holding out with the idiotic hope that although they would never be anything more, that they could have at least been friends.

MAY 30, 1953

JUNE HAD been away for work since the twentieth and he could think of nothing but curling into bed and sleeping for at least a day. He had not gone to seen clients, he had been called away by his king to help him conduct his otherworldly business.

This time, it had been tending to a half dozen whelping hell beasts. It had been a long, tiring process and he had been bitten eight times, not counting all the nips he'd gotten from the pups.

His king had personally tended to each bite, thanking June often and sincerely.

"What do you need these things for anyways?" June had asked him after bite number seven.

His king had pressed his mouth to the bite, which stung, but turned it from wound to scab. "Oh, they have their purpose. It's not all scheming, you know, I do have an entire realm of sinners to punish."

"They're very ill-tempered."

"They don't bite me," the Devil had said with a smile.

"Well, you're Satan and I'm just some low-level minion."

"Junius!" he'd scolded. "Don't say things like that, you know I love you."

"I know."

"What's wrong?" he'd asked, running a hand along June's face.

June had wrapped his arms around him, pressing hard. "I want to go home." He hadn't meant to start crying, but he had, burying his face in his king's chest.

"Oh, shh, I know, we all do."

"I'm sorry, I know...it's not your fault, I just...I want to go home so bad."

"And I'll bring you there, as soon as I can, don't worry," he'd promised. He'd wiped away June's tears. "No more crying, I hate to see you cry."

"I love you."

"I love you, too," the Devil had said, "And I know I owe you so much more than what I've given you."

June had shaken his head.

"You know that, right? That I call upon you when I need you, but that if you need me, you are to do the same."

"Yes."

"Promise?"

June had nodded and said, "Yes."

"Ohh! That must be Shelia screaming, are you ready to get back in there?" he'd asked.

June had nodded. Of course, Shelia had bitten him too. His hands and arms were still laced with scabs from their bites. He tossed his coat on the arm of the couch and sat down, grabbing the blanket that draped over the back and pulling it onto his lap.

He saw a pile of mail on his coffee table and thought about ignoring it until he saw a letter on the top. He reached for it, hoping it would be one of the happy, thankful letters he received from new parents.

"You don't know how hard I had to try not to read that," Wei said from the kitchen.

"You still here?" June asked.

"Sure, I'm worried about you. Wanted t'check in. Look, all your plants still alive. Aren't y'proud of me?"

"Very."

"It's from your vampire," Wei said. "Be a love and read it out loud."

"No."

"June!"

June sighed and opened the letter.

Wei came and sat beside him, peering over his shoulder. "Dear June."

"Cut it out."

Carefully enunciating in his best American accent, Wei read, "I have tried to call you since we last saw each other, but I couldn't even make myself dial the phone. I owe you an apology. What I said was incredibly rude, intentionally hurtful, and I'm very sorry. If I knew a better word than sorry, I'd be that too."

"Wei, stop," June said, trying to pull the letter out of his sight, but Wei had his hand wrapped around June's.

"Stop it, June, you know I can't see out of that eye," he said, pulling June's hand back into his line of vision. He continued, "I hope you understand that what I said was said out of fear. Not of you, of course, you've been nothing but kind to me. It's no excuse to say that things have been hard for me lately, between Annie and this change in lifestyle."

"He doesn't even sound like that, you're making him sound like he's from Ohio."

"Well, I'm rubbish at New York accents. I hope you can understand, at least, if not forgive me. I hope we can remain friends, although if it were impossible, I would understand. Deepest apologies, James Kelly."

June sighed.

"P.S. I dream about you every night, I touch myself when I think of you. I want you, hard and—"

"Wei, stop it, he didn't write that!" June said, yanking his hand away. He tossed the letter on the table.

Wei grinned, but June felt no amusement.

"It came a few days ago, anyways, that letter. You should let him know you got it, even if you don't accept it. What happened t'your arm?"

"Shelia."

"Who's Shelia and is she single?"

"Shelia is a hell beast."

"Well, alright, but I mean...is she...sort of person-shaped?"

"No."

"Right, then, never mind. Anyways, I should get home, less you need me t'stay?"

"No, thanks, though."

"You want me t'send Micah back over?"

"No."

Wei patted his back and pet Gordon goodbye.

June sat on the couch for a quarter hour, thinking, until he picked up the phone and dialed James Kelly's number.

"Hello?" the vampire answered.

June almost hung up. "I got your letter."

"June?"

"Mhm."

"Oh. I'm, uh...you read it?"

"Of course, I did."

"I just...I feel awful about what I said, I know I always give you a hard time about that and I really shouldn't have said that."

"I figure you shouldn't have."

"It was...I don't know, I want to make excuses, but there aren't any."

"Yeah, well, you know, don't do it again."

"I won't."

Neither said anything for a while.

June cleared his throat and asked, "You've been doing okay on your circuit?"

"Yes."

"Good, I'm glad to hear that." They both went quiet again, so June said, "Anyways, I'll let you go."

"Sure, but...you know, don't be a stranger."

"Sure."

"Goodbye, June."

"Bye."

June hung up and looked at Gordon, who had come over to chew on some of his mail. He flapped a hand at the cat and Gordon just looked at him. He picked up the cat and held him close to his chest.

"At least you can't talk," he said.

For a moment, he wondered what he would do if Gordon spoke back to him, but the cat only purred.

He picked up the phone again and called Wei.

"Lo?" Wei answered.

"Is Micah single?"

"What?"

"Is he seeing anyone?"

"He's a whore, June, he's seeing a lot of people."

"I know, I don't care."

"I'm not letting you take him off the market."

"I don't care if he still works for you."

"June."

"It doesn't matter, I don't care who he sleeps with or how

many people he sleeps with," June said, "Just...I don't know, see if he'd want to go on a date sometime. Unpaid, totally voluntary."

"I'll ask him, I'll call you back in ten."

"Thanks."

June, for two minutes, waited patiently. After that, he began to pace the house and worry about what a stupid question he had asked.

The phone rang and he snatched it up. "So?" he asked.

"He says no thanks."

"Oh."

"It's...he says he's not interested in somefin like that right now. He wanted me t'make sure you know it's not to do wif you, though. He says you're nice."

"Thanks."

"I'm sorry, June."

"It was just a whim. It doesn't matter."

"Y'need anyfing, just let me know."

"Thanks. I'm alright, though."

They hung up and June lay down on the couch, lacking the will to get up and go to bed. Gordon curled up on top of him, purring and kneading him from time to time. Maybe, June thought, all he needed was more pets. It was not that he had trouble finding someone to sleep with, it was that he had trouble finding someone to keep. Pets had no choice in the matter, they lived where they were brought.

Maybe he would get another cat and a dog and some rabbits and fill his apartment with little souls that needed him so that it didn't matter if the men he slept with were only friends or acquaintances.

JUNE 8, 1953

JUNE HAD his arm wrapped around a man whose name he believed to be Paul. Or maybe Peter. He wasn't sure and didn't care. Peter was human, mostly. He was blood bonded to a vampire that June knew had been in the city for twenty or so years; he and Paul-or-Peter had spoken in passing before but never noticed much of each other.

Except, that night, in the bar, June had noticed that when he smiled, crinkles appeared around his eyes.

"What's your name again?" June asked.

"Simon."

"Hmm."

"What?"

June shook his head. "Doesn't matter. Where are we going?"

"I told you, my place is around here," Paul said, his arm tight around June so that the creature felt safe.

"Mmm, won't your vampire mind?"

"Regina doesn't mind much," Simon assured.

June felt, vaguely, that that couldn't be true, but he'd been drinking and was not thinking clearly, somewhat deliberately. "What do you like, Simon?" he asked.

"What?"

"What do you like to do in bed?"

Simon turned to look at him and pressed his mouth to June's.

"Wait until I show you."

June melted against him, reaching up to slide his arms around the man's neck.

"Hey, not out here, though, someone will see," Simon said, taking June's arms from around him. "A few more blocks."

June followed, feeling hazy but excited, down the street and up the stairs to a third-floor apartment. Holding on to Simon's hand, he allowed himself to be brought into a dimly lit apartment.

A woman sat in an armchair in the corner; she looked up when they entered.

"Regina, look what I found."

She stood and came over, circling around June, her eyes scanning him. "How unique."

"I, uh...I'm not much interested in women like that," June said.

Simon slipped an arm around June's waist, holding him from behind. Into his ear, he said softly, "You don't mind, though, if she watches, do you?"

"Um..." June thought about it. He didn't know if he minded.

"We can give it a try, right?" Simon asked, one arm still around him, pressing against his back, the other caressing June between the legs, getting him hard. "I'll be so good to you that you won't even notice. That's okay, right?"

June sighed and leaned deeper into Simon's embrace. "Yes."

The man turned him around and kissed him again. He moved June over to the couch and straddled him, covering him with kisses and touches.

Every so often June would glance over at the woman and after the third time, Simon said, "Shh, I know what to do."

He produced a piece of silk and wound it around June's eyes and kissed him again, stifling any protest he might have voiced. A moment later, Simon's comfortable weight was gone and June worried for a second until he felt the man pulling his trousers and underwear down. He lifted his lips to help and moaned when he felt Simon's hand on him, caressing him tenderly along the thighs.

He took June into his mouth and June surrendered himself to the experience, focusing on the sensation instead of worrying about the blindfold. Minutes passed and June found himself blissful and content until he felt something on his arm, another hand and then a pair of lips. He was not very concerned until a sharp pain shot up his arm.

"Hey!" he said, pulling his arm back and sitting up straighter.

The movement must have startled Simon, because he pulled back abruptly, his teeth scraping against June.

The demon tore at the blindfold and saw Regina had come over to the couch and bitten him.

"I didn't say that was okay," he said.

"Hold him," Regina said to Simon.

June scrambled over towards the arm of the couch, his legs tangled in the clothing around his ankles. Simon grabbed him.

"Stop it," the demon insisted.

"I'm sorry," Simon said, "Most people don't notice. She only wants a little bit."

"*No*," June said, "Are you out of your mind?"

Regina reached for his arm again and he yanked it back.

"Shh," Simon said, his hand back between June's legs, caressing him. "I'll make it so you don't notice."

"Stop it," June said, his heart in his throat. "*Stop!*"

When Simon didn't stop, June shoved his hand away and pushed him. His mobility was compromised badly and he thought for a moment that they would be able to abuse him any way they wanted. Simon reached for him, this time to grab his hand, and June grabbed him first, his claws extending.

He pressed the points of his claws into Simon's wrist and said, "Get off of me or I'll gut so you can't be put back together."

Simon looked at Regina.

"Do you know what I am?" June asked, "I am malak ha-satan, among the first fallen, and I have seen the beasts that await you if you harm me. An eternity of punishment if you don't let me go now."

Regina released his arm and Simon tried to pull his hand away. June let him go and grabbed his pants, pulling them back up as quickly as he could, not caring that they were bunched and crooked. As soon as his belt was fastened, he went for the door, feeling sick.

He ran down the stairs and, outside, a woman sitting on a piece of cardboard gave him a funny look. He glanced down at himself and saw that he did look concerning, disheveled and untucked.

"Someone's husband come home?" she asked.

He shrugged.

"Got any change?"

He reached into his pocket and pulled out the change he'd

gotten when he'd paid for his drinks. A few dollars, not a fortune, but what he had on him. He handed it over.

"Thanks."

He lit a cigarette and when he saw her staring at it, handed it over then lit another one for himself.

"Thanks again. You're bleeding, you know."

He looked down at his arm and sighed. "You got somewhere to go tonight?" he asked.

"No."

"Come with me."

She frowned. "Why?"

"Because I only sleep with men and you're pregnant."

"I'm not."

He nodded. "I promise, you are," he said, pointing to his horns. "It's kind of my deal."

She shook her head again, but this time it seemed to be an action of defeat, not denial. "I can't..."

"Come on," he said. He put a hand on her shoulder and guided her along. "What's your name?"

"Kathy."

"Don't worry, Kathy," he said. "We'll get things all figured out for you. Sound good?"

She nodded, taking another drag on her cigarette. The action was automatic, almost robotic.

"What are you doing out here?" he asked.

She shrugged. "Nowhere to go, not good enough at anything to keep a job," she said in a harsh, hateful way that made June think that there was more going on. "Don't look at me that way."

"Sorry." He looked at his watch and thought about how long it would take to get from Highbridge to his apartment; he was still drunk, as well as jittery from Simon and Regina's attempt. Normally, he had trouble getting cabs, especially if he was outside of Manhattan, where he was better known to the human residents.

He resigned himself to the subway.

"Do you have parents, or friends, maybe?"

"Parents live in Colorado," she said, "Thought I'd come out here and get a new start, find a job, meet a nice guy. Like they show in the movies."

"Well, you met someone," he said.

"He's *not* a nice guy."

"Guess not, no."

"Listen, I don't want to talk about any of this," she said, "I shouldn't even be going with you."

"Something to eat and a shower, then," June said, "I won't make you stay."

She shook her head at him. "I don't even know why I believe you."

"Mothers trust me," he said with a shrug. He looked down at his arm and knew the shirt was ruined. His throat tightened and he cleared his throat, saying, "Anyways, there's a station up here."

Once inside, he showed Kathy the bathroom and told her to make herself at home. He then went to the phone and dialed up Gertie.

"It better be good," she answered.

"You've got poachers."

"Junius?"

"That's me. Anyways, a vampire in Highbridge has something sketchy going on. Her blood bond is bringing back people without getting permission to drink."

"Oh, hold on, let me get a pen."

He waited.

"Alright, go ahead. Names."

"Regina and Simon. If you've had a lot of men going missing...well, I think you should look into it."

"Sure, thanks for letting me know. Who tipped you?"

He looked down at his arm. "Uh. She bit me."

Gertie's voice went hard. "I'll deal with her."

"Thanks. Don't go too harsh...you know, unless you need to."

"You deal with Manhattan, I'll handle the Bronx. How's that Brooklyn vampire of yours doing?"

He sighed. "He's not mine, I was just helping him out. He lives here, anyways, not in Brooklyn, so it's my business to help him out."

"Sure," she said.

"Anyways, I've got to go." He hung up and examined his arm again. He threw the shirt away and pressed a clean towel to the bite. It wasn't very deep, but he wondered what she would have done if he hadn't noticed.

Gordon meowed at him and he checked the food bowl, saw that it was emptied and filled it. He looked at all of his plants and found them in good health.

Kathy emerged from the bathroom holding the robe June had offered her. "I washed up a little."

"You can shower if you want."

She shrugged. "No towels."

"I'll get you a towel. Are you hungry?" he asked.

"You don't—"

"Hungry or not?" he asked.

"Yes."

He went to the linen closet, took a towel and handed it to her. "Alright, shower, I'll make something."

She pursed her lips, but turned and went back into the bathroom.

In the kitchen, June set the coffee pot and started to make an omelet. His hands shook a little as he cracked the eggs and he imagined they were unsteady due to the drinking he'd done until he dropped one of the eggs and began to cry as he stared at it on the floor.

He wiped his eyes with the back of his wrist and knelt, trying to sop up the egg with a hand towel as Gordon licked at it.

"Gordon, stop!" he said, pushing the cat away.

Gordon ignored him, twisting around June and going back to the egg. He pushed the cat away again and wiped up the mess, throwing the whole towel in the garbage. He continued to sniffle and tried to crack another egg, but ended up with more shells in the bowl than egg.

He sat down on the floor after that, pulling his knees to his chest and resting his head on his knees. Tears and snot dribbled down his face and Gordon rubbed against his legs.

He looked up when Kathy cleared her throat from the doorway between the kitchen and the living room.

"You, uh...you need something?" she asked.

He wiped his face again and shook his head. "No. Sorry. I'm a horrible mess, just ignore me." He stood up and rubbed his eyes, picked the egg shells out of the bowl and carried on making the omelet for her.

She stood in the doorway and he said, "Go on and have a seat."

"You sure you're alright?" she asked.

"Yes," he lied.

The omelet didn't take long to make and he served it to her with toast and coffee. He washed the dishes to keep himself occupied while she ate and once he ran out of things to wash, he felt his throat start to ache again.

He coughed and Kathy looked at him again. "Why don't you make yourself some coffee?"

He felt very stupid that the idea hadn't occurred to him before. Once he had his drink, he sat at the kitchen table across from her.

"So," he said once he'd burned his tongue.

"What?"

"What do you want to do?"

"About what?"

"Are you ready to be a mom?"

"No," she said.

"I can help with that," he said, "I can help with whatever you decide."

"I'm not ready to decide anything," she said.

"You want to tell the father?"

"I don't know."

"That's okay, take your time and think. If you want to keep or end it or put it for adoption, whatever you decide, I can help. You can stay here for a while if you need."

She stared into her coffee and then looked up at him. "Thank you. You didn't need to do any of this."

"It's my job to help," he said.

"What's your name anyways?"

"Junius Thompson. Most people call me June," he said. "You look beat, I'll make up the couch for you. It's a pullout and I think it's pretty comfortable."

She followed him to the linen closet and helped him make the bed once he'd moved the coffee table out of the way and pulled the mattress out. He got her settled and went to his own room, where he sat on his bed, alone with his thoughts, thinking of Simon and Regina, wondering what they could have done to him and feeling very stupid and mildly sick. He sat like that for a while, in the dark, until tears overcame him again and he buried his face in a pillow to try to stifle the noise.

JUNE 12, 1953

HAVING COMPANY other than Gordon and his plants had improved June's life; Kathy gave him someone to talk to and care for. He cooked for her and did his best to make her smile; today he had brought her home job applications for every business with which he had a connection. He handed her the sheaf of papers and said, "You said you couldn't make any choices until you had a job."

She stared up at him.

"So pick which one and fill it out," he said. "There's a little note on each one about the job."

"Just one?" she asked.

He nodded. "Don't worry, I have connections."

"I'm not any good at keeping a job, I'll just lose it."

"You can't give up," he said.

She sighed and started to leaf through the papers, peering at the notes he had jotted on each application. "You went and got all of these today?"

He nodded.

"Thank you. You didn't need to."

"Maybe I just want you off my couch," he said, giving her a smile.

She smiled back. "Your friend called."

"Which one?"

"The Chinese fellow."

"Wei," he said, "His name's Wei."

She nodded.

"What did he want?"

"He asked for you to call him back."

"Thanks," he said and went to the phone.

Wei picked up after two rings and said, "Lo."

"You called."

"I did! Y'want t'make a hundred dollars this comin Tuesday?"

"What?"

"Yeah, I got a lady who fancies somefin a bit different."

"Women aren't much my speed, Wei, you know that."

"Aye, but that's the good part, she don't want anyfin...you know...sexual. She wants t'show you off."

"I don't know, Wei."

"You'd be doing me a real favor," he said. "She's a proper good client."

June looked out the window and thought for a while; Wei sounded desperate and June liked to do people favors when he could. "You promise she won't expect anything from me?"

"No, just to look interesting and act like a gentleman."

"Alright, I guess."

"Oh, June, you've saved me again."

"I do what I can."

"I really do love you. Write this down."

June got a pen and waited.

"Tuesday, seven thirty, meet her at her apartment building. Black tie. Her husband might be there but don't engage him. You writing this?"

"Yes. Where am I supposed to meet her?"

"At her apartment building, June, I just told you!"

"You have to tell me her address."

"Oh, bugger, sorry," Wei said, "She lives in the Dakota."

"No."

"Aye."

"You know, I haven't got anything to wear to this," he said.

"Good thing we're just about the same size," Wei said. "I'll bring over something for you. You're a life saver."

"Mm."

"Thank you, I love you, I've got to go," Wei said. "I've a million other things t'do."

June smiled. "Bye."

He went to sit on the couch but paused when he got there. It was still pulled out as a bed. Kathy looked at him and said, "Sorry, I can pick it up if you want."

"No, that's fine."

"Is he your boyfriend?" she asked.

"Who?"

"That Chinese fellow."

"What's his name again?"

She sighed. "Wei. Do you and him go around together?"

"No, Wei doesn't like men. He's a friend. Why?"

"Just when he came over the other day, he was very...you know. Friendly."

He grinned. "A friend being friendly? Can't imagine."

"You know what I meant."

"I know exactly what you meant," June said. He sat on the coffee table and picked up the watch that sat next to his mail.

"Found it under the couch, the cat was trying to get it," Kathy said.

He didn't recognize it; he flipped it over and saw the initials JKJR. He frowned at it for a moment, then reached for the phone.

"Hello?" Anastasia answered.

"Is James Kelly around?"

"He is."

"Can I speak with him?"

"One moment," she answered, her voice clipped.

Half a minute later, James Kelly said, "Hello?"

"Hi. It's me. June."

"I know."

"What's your middle name?"

"Jacob."

"James Kelly Jacob?" June asked.

"Yes. Why?"

"Are you missing a watch?"

"I am."

"You left it here. Kathy found it under the couch."

"Oh," he said, and then asked, "Who's Kathy?"

"Don't worry about who's Kathy. You want to come by to pick it up?"

"Wednesday? Annie and I are going away for a little bit, taking a trip, you know?"

"Somewhere nice?" June asked, suspecting that they were trying to patch things up with a vacation.

"Yes."

"Alright, well, come by Wednesday then. I'll see you."

"Bye."

Smiling to himself, the demon added, "And no chewing on any of the other tourists while you're away."

"I'll be fine," he said and June liked that it sounded confident instead of unsure.

LATE TUESDAY afternoon, Wei brought by two sets of formal wear for June to try on, in slightly different sizes, as well as an envelope that contained one hundred dollars in mixed bills. As June put the envelope into his rainy day fund on top of the fridge, Wei looked him over. "You're a bit wider than I am these days," he said. "The bigger one is a little old, but how much can a tux change?"

"Mm."

"I brought a waistcoat, I think they look smarter," he said, handing the larger outfit over to June. "Go try it on and we'll do somefin wif your hair."

"What's wrong with my hair?"

"Have y'got your own shoes?"

"Yes."

The man said, "They've got to be black."

"Wei, evening dress hasn't changed much since Queen Victoria, I got my black shoes all polished and nice this morning."

"I love you, go get dressed."

Kathy looked between them and June took the clothes Wei had brought into the bedroom. He heard Wei ask her, "So you still here then?" but didn't listen for her response.

He shimmied into the clothes Wei had brought, going immediately for the larger size. Wei had slimmed down in years past and though they were nearly the same height, June had a broader frame.

He looked at himself in the mirror and adjusted his clothes a little. He felt good and he looked good, too. He smiled. He stepped out of his room and spread his arms so Wei could examine him.

"What do you think?"

Wei circled around him and nodded. He touched June's face, tilting it from side to side. "What a good face that bugger up in heaven gave you. But what about your hair..." He reached up to run his fingers through June's dark gray hair, unruly as always.

"It's hard to comb it right," he said, touching his pale gray horns. "They get in the way..."

"Leave it," Kathy said.

Wei turned to look at her.

"Leave his hair," she said. "It's...contrast, right? The messy hair and the horns against the tails. Like black against white."

Wei looked back at June, thinking. "Alright, yeah, might work."

"Why you so worked up about this woman anyways?" June asked.

"She's got a lot of pull with the folks I'm in wif," he said.

"Are you in trouble?"

"Eh...not as of yet," he said, rubbing the back of his neck. "All you got to do is be exotic for a night, yeah?"

"Sure. You'd let me know if you were in trouble, wouldn't you?"

"Why? Would you call up Great-granddad and get me out of this?" Wei asked.

"I'll do whatever I can."

June looked at the clock. He had time to eat beforehand; he didn't know if there would even be food.

Wei saw him look at the kitchen and said, "Don't you dare cook in that."

"Oh, calm down, I've got time to change out and back in. Are you going to stay and fret?"

Wei nodded.

June shook his head.

He changed, ate and changed back; at just before seven he headed out the door with Kathy and Wei bidding him farewell.

The doorman at the Dakota allowed him in, giving him a look-over and saying, "Are you Mrs. Freeman's guest?"

"Did she tell you to look out for someone funny looking?"

"Unusual," the doorman said. "You may wait in the lobby for Mrs. Freeman. She will be down shortly."

"Thanks." He sat on one of the couches and folded his hands on his lap. At one minute before seven-thirty, a woman came over to him.

"Are you my guest?" she asked.

He looked up to see a handsome woman, a few years past forty, in a full-length evening gown in a shade of plum that June found deeply appealing.

"Wei sent me," he said, not sure how else to answer.

She nodded. "Well, let's go."

He stood and offered her his arm.

"How gracious. There's a car waiting outside for us, or there certainly should be."

He nodded and escorted her out the door, then opened the door of the town car for her. Once inside the vehicle, he said, "I remember when they used to make these with the fronts open. Is this a Cadillac?"

"It is."

June felt proud; he had a hard time telling cars apart, as they were all roaring beasts to him. He had taken a ride in the Model-T and had been put off ever since.

"I'm not so young that I don't remember how town cars used to be," she said. "You're not trying to flatter me, are you?"

"No, but you are very young to me," he said.

She gave him a smile and looked him over again. "Wei did not mention what you are, or your name."

"Junius Thompson, malak ha-satan, among the first fallen," he said.

"What a mouthful."

"Most people call me June."

"You may call me Lillian."

"And not Lily, I expect."

"No," she said, "Not Lily."

"Where are we headed?"

"Oh, just a little gathering," she said, looking out the window. "At Hotel Elysée. I don't imagine you've ever been there before?"

"Not since Tallulah Bankhead threw that party," he said.

"You know Tallulah Bankhead?"

"Sure," he said, "Slept with some of the same people."

Lillian laughed at that, turning her eyes back to him. "I think you'll do excellently with my friends tonight."

"I hope so."

The driver let them out of the car and June offered Lillian his arm again. They walked in and June glanced around at the hotel, recalling days when the castles of lords had rushes on the floors. As he thought of the smell, he counted indoor plumbing as one of the world's true miracles.

Lillian put a glass of champagne in his hand and introduced him to a lot of a people. Most of them wanted to touch his horns and some of them even asked before they did it. He listened to the questions he was asked with mild attention, listening to the piano that played on the other side of the room with more interest.

One woman grabbed his free hand and he looked at her.

"Your nails...are they...I mean, do they come out like cat's claws?" she asked, rubbing the pad of her thumb over his nail, then touching the tip.

"Yes."

Her eyes snapped to his face, then back to his hand. "Show me."

He extracted his hand from her grip, not wanting to cause harm, and extended his claws to their full length. She grabbed his hand again and he warned, "Careful, they're sharp you know."

"What have you got claws for anyways?" the man beside her asked.

"The standard things, I suppose," he said, "Scratching, fighting, marking territory. Not a lot of call for that these days, though."

A waiter came over and exchanged his empty glass for a full one.

The process repeated several times as the hours went on; the exchange of questions and answers, the exchange of glasses. As the nonconsensual touching of his horns, skin and claws continued, June considered asking Wei for more money and definitely knew he would never do this kind of favor again. He realized he had not asked how long this party would last.

"What a pair of eyes," one man said, putting his hand on June's face and tilting it towards the light so his eye color could be seen better.

June flinched at being grabbed like that. He wanted to say something, but his tongue felt heavy and swollen in his mouth. It had grown dimmer in the room and he looked around, frowning. He set his champagne glass down and rubbed his eyes.

"Are you feeling alright?" Lillian asked, but something rang false in her voice. "Have a seat."

He sat, her hands pushing him into the chair, feeling more like catcher's mitts than the hands of a woman. He squeezed his eyes shut for a moment.

"Something," he said.

"I know, don't worry," she said.

The man beside her took something silver from his pockets and clasped them around June's wrists. Someone slipped their arms under his arms and hefted him out of his chair; another person took his legs.

"I thought the pills would never take," a voice said.

The lights had gone very dim now, except for a circle of candlelight around a table in the middle of the room.

June flopped uselessly in the arms of the two who carried him. They set him up on the table and secured his arms above his head.

Two dozen faces peered down at him and he heard the fuzzy voices of dozens more. The people who had prodded and caressed him through the night.

He shook his head sluggishly from side to side, trying to say something, but doing no more than moaning.

"Are you sure this will work?" someone asked. "None of the others did."

"It had to be interesting," Lillian said, "And virgins, no matter how pretty, just aren't interesting."

June hated that word. Virgin. A nonsense word for something that didn't matter.

A pair of hands reached forward and traced over his face with a paintbrush that reeked of wormwood and lavender.

"Up," June said.

"Shh," Lillian soothed.

"Gonthrup," he said.

They ignored him and someone began to chant. Another came at him with a knife, causing June's stomach to churn harder, and stuck him in the belly. He cried out and their voices quieted; the candles guttered, then flared and they all gasped and whispered when a new body joined them.

A slight man with dandelion colored skin appeared at the head of the table and June stared up at a childlike face haloed with peach colored curls.

"June?" the man asked.

June opened his mouth and a lot of spit dribbled out. He

moaned.

"Oh, June, no," the man said.

"Kaveon, lord of pleas—" Lillian began.

Kaveon grabbed her by the throat. "You did this?" he asked.

"We seek what you can offer us and present this man in exchange. He will please you," she said.

The creature they had summoned tightened his hand around her throat, squeezing until she couldn't even choke out a sound. The others all stared, some backing away, others screaming and a handful fainting. June felt a small pleasure to see that one of the men who had grabbed his horns and pulled on them to see if they were real was among the ones that fainted. He hoped he hit his head hard.

Kaveon dropped Lillian when she had gone limp but before she died. "Get out, all of you," he said.

They went, hurrying and tripping over each other, shoving and fighting like hungry dogs over a scrap.

Kaveon undid June's bonds and pulled open his shirt, saying, "I'm sorry, June, I've got to take a look, make sure it's not too bad."

June understood what he said but moaned anyways when he felt a hand on him. Feather light touches felt like blows.

"Oh, Junie, not so bad. Here hold this to you..."

"Can," he mumbled, his hands not working enough to hold the folded tablecloth against his wound. "Can't."

"Okay, don't worry," Kaveon said, taking another table cloth and tying it over the folded one. June cried each time he was moved and the other creature murmured an apology each time. "You still live in the same place?"

June nodded.

"Okay, I'm going to take you home. Hold on if you can," he said. Kaveon lifted June, his thin arms stronger than they looked.

"Tired."

"Try not to do that," Kaveon said.

June's head leaned against the other creature's chest. "Keys pocket," he said and after that, there was nothing.

JUNE WOKE feeling sore and weighted down. He heard Kathy, Wei, and Kaveon talking in the other room. He peered down at his chest to see that part of the heaviness in his body could be attributed to the cat sleeping on him, purring peacefully.

He reached up and rubbed the top of the cat's head; with a small sound, the cat opened his eyes and looked at June. Gordon stood and stretched, then walked away, stepping directly onto the place where June had been stabbed.

He cried out and three people rushed through his door.

"I'm so sorry," Wei said immediately. "I am, I had no idea."

"I know," June said, pushing himself up to sit.

"I really—"

"Wei, I know," he said.

"I was going to call in the big guns if you didn't wake up soon," Kaveon said.

"I'm fine."

"I need you around, you know," he said. "Sex without fertility? It'd be a nasty mess."

"Don't worry, I'm not dead," he said.

Kaveon came over and brushed his hair out of his face. He rubbed his cheek with his thumb. "I hate that we got back together like this."

"Yeah," June said. "How's Liz?"

Kaveon ran his hand through his own hair and said, "Good."

"And how's baby Eddy?"

"Near to three hundred now, not much of a baby," Kaveon said.

"We really haven't kept in touch," June said.

The doorbell rang.

"What day is it?" June asked.

"Wednesday," Kathy answered.

"Oh! That'll be James Kelly, someone let him in, he's here to get his watch."

Kathy went and June pushed himself up more.

"What are you doing?" Wei asked.

"He gets weird if I'm naked," June said, reaching for a bathrobe and dragging his feet off the side of the bed.

"June."

"Oh, a bit of drugging and stabbing and you get so worried," June scolded. "Georgia was worse."

"Doesn't mean I like it," Wei said.

June pulled on his robe and stood, arranging it around himself and tying it shut. Kathy had let James Kelly in by the time June had shuffled out to the living room. The vampire looked up from petting Gordon, frowned and then asked, "Am I interrupting something?"

"No."

James Kelly eyed Kaveon warily. "Alright. Anyways, thanks for finding my watch. I've had it since my bar mitzvah."

June leaned gingerly over the coffee table and lifted the watch. He held it out to the vampire, who took it and fastened it around his wrist.

"You, uh. June, you don't look good."

"I'm the cat's whiskers, don't worry," June said.

"If you say so, you look like death."

"Death would be very upset to hear you say that," Kaveon said, smiling at James Kelly in a way that June knew was meant to make his belly tighten and skin warm.

He smacked the other creature in the arm with the back of his hand and said, "Leave him alone."

"Oh, just a little playing, June," Kaveon said, "You know I like to play with things."

"I'll go, I think I did interrupt something," James Kelly said.

"You don't have to," June said.

"You look like you need rest," the vampire said. "Give me a call if you're feeling better."

June nodded and James Kelly saw himself out. Once the door closed, June pushed Kaveon. "Why do you always do that?"

The man shrugged. "I like to tease and he wants someone to tease him."

"He wants to be left alone," June said snapped, "He's got a girl. Don't go messing around with things."

"Still sore, then, I guess," Kaveon said.

"Guess so."

"I said I was sorry."

"I know. Doesn't make it better."

A yellow hand brushed through peach curls. "Anyways, I think you're through the worst of it now. I'll check in with you in a few days."

"You don't need to."

"But I will," he said. "I cared about you before and I still care about you, June."

June shrugged. "Thanks."

"Feel better."

June nodded.

Kaveon let himself out.

"That's him, then," Wei said.

"Shh."

"That's who?" Kathy asked.

Wei answered, "His ex."

"Wei, shut up."

"Go back to bed, I'll back you something to eat," Kathy said.

"I want a bath," June said.

"Alright, a bath, then bed, then you'll eat," she said.

He soaked for a long time in the bath, running his fingers over his newest scar. The skin had healed over already but remained tender and very sore. He suspected that his insides would need a while before they healed entirely. His wounds had been made to heal like that, quick on the outside and slower on the inside. He didn't know why they couldn't heal quick all over.

Of course, he reflected, when this body had been made, it had been little more than a temporary form, made for trips to earth, to be discarded when he returned to heaven.

He ran a claw over the scar, sending little bolts of pain through himself, and wondered how hard he would have to press to open it again.

Someone knocked and he said, "You can come it."

Wei entered and crouched beside the bath. "June, I can't even tell you—"

"Don't tell me anything," he said.

"I'm sorry."

June sighed. "I'm not mad, you're forgiven, I love you, whatever you need to hear."

"You're too good," he said. "Kathy says your food is almost done."

"Alright." He sat up a little and winced.

Wei reached out and took his arm, helping him up and wrapping him in a towel. "Now that you're awake, though, I—"

"Have to go?"

"Sorry."

"It's fine. You've got a job and you've got kids, I understand. I'm a big boy, I'll be okay. Not to mention, I don't think Kathy's going anywhere."

Wei stayed long enough to help him dry and dress. He said goodbye with a long hug and another apology.

Once he settled into bed, Kathy brought him food and sat on the edge of his bed while he ate.

"Is this a normal sort of thing for you?" she asked.

"No."

"You don't seem phased."

"I don't know," he said. "Maybe I've been around too long for anything to phase me."

She gave him a look that told him she knew he was lying.

"I don't know what to tell you, Kath, I'll be crying later I'm sure. Have you made any choices yet? About being a mom or a job?"

She nodded. "I'm going to have the baby. If I can hold down a job, I'll keep it, if not, I want you to find a better home for it."

He smiled.

"If I hadn't been meant to be a mother to this child, you wouldn't have found me."

"What?"

"If I'd still been out there, without you giving me all these chances...but we found each other, and I think that means something."

He didn't know what to say to that, so he nodded.

"You done eating?"

"Yeah, thanks, I think I want to go back to sleep."

She took his plate and left him. He pulled his covers up and wrapped his arms around one of the pillows, wishing he had someone to hold. He didn't like that recently this was what had haunted his thoughts, the longing to hold someone and love them, to be allowed to run his hands through someone else's hair and press his lips to their skin.

Seeing Kaveon had not helped because although centuries had passed, it still stung to see him. He remembered the day Kaveon had sat down with him, clasping one of June's hands between both of his.

"June...do you remember that you told me you don't care if I lie with other people?" he'd asked.

"Kavi, I've *watched* you lie with other people, of course, I don't care," he'd said, smiling. "That's not what love is about, not for me."

"There's a girl, June, and she wants more. And I do, too, with her."

June had looked at him for a while and thought. An idea had come to him and he'd said, "She can come to live with us. I'd like to have a girl around. We can be friends."

"No."

That word had set his guts twisting. "Why not?"

"That's not what she wants. And it's not what I want."

"She wants you to choose?"

Kaveon had nodded.

"And you choose her?" June had asked.

"I do."

"Kavi."

"It's been great with you, June, and I care about you, I really do."

"But you care about her more."

"We're having a baby."

"I like babies."

"June, it's about more than that. You know it is."

"Please, don't, Kavi. I love you," June had said, reaching out with his other hand to hold Kaveon's hands, as though holding on physically could make him change his mind.

"I love you, too, June, I do, but not like that. Not anymore. I'm sorry."

Gordon jumped up to nestle next to June, pulling him out of his memories. "Hi, Gordon," he said. He ran his fingers along the cat's spine and Gordon began to purr. "You always come home, though, don't you?"

"Are you talking to yourself?" Kathy asked through the door.

"To the cat," he called.

"That's fine then," she said.

He wondered if he had been loud or if she had been listening. He continued to pet the cat and the repetition, along with Gordon's purrs, lulled him to sleep.

In the morning, someone knocked on his bedroom door and Kathy called, "That fellow is back."

"Wei?" he asked.

"No, the Negro."

He pulled himself out of bed, disturbing Gordon, and went to the living room, where James Kelly stood giving Kathy a sour look. He had a grocery bag in his arms.

"Did you bother to ask his name, Kathy?" June asked.

She walked away to the kitchen without answering.

"Sorry," June said, "You know white people. We're working on her."

"You working on all of them?" James Kelly asked, giving a small smile.

"As best I can. Anyways, what brings you around?"

"You really did look sick yesterday, I thought maybe I should bring by something to make you feel better."

June grinned. "Thanks."

James Kelly offered him the bag and June took it, peering inside to see several containers of soup. He couldn't stop smiling.

"Sorry about cutting out so fast, I just...you know."

"Got nervous? Felt sort of hot and excited? Yeah, he does that on purpose."

"Is he what you are?"

"Fallen? Yes. Do you want to come in or do you have somewhere to be?" June asked.

"What do you mean he does it on purpose?"

"I get things fertile, he gets them horny," June said. "Spring was always busy for us, you should have seen Babylon. Ishtar knew how to have a party."

"An angel for fertility I can buy."

"But not for sex?" June asked. "Who do you think all those husbands with a handful of wives were lighting candles to? Or how about the wives? If you're one out of three hundred concubines with nothing around but eunuchs, what do you think your chances are? I mean...there's always the other concubines...but that's off topic. I was thanking you for the soup."

"You're welcome."

"And I asked if you wanted to stay."

"For a little while, I can."

"Good," June said and walked into the kitchen. He set the bag on the counter and set up the coffee. He sat at the kitchen table and James Kelly folded his hands on the table; June suspected it was to keep them from fidgeting.

For a while, neither said anything, until James Kelly blurted, "Does that mean he makes you feel it, the way you do?"

"What?"

"That other demon, the yellow one. Did he make me feel what I did? I mean, put the thoughts there?"

"Not...it's complicated with him, he can get you to do things you normally wouldn't, but only because on some level you want to do it. He couldn't make me sleep with a girl, for instance."

The vampire looked uneasy. "You're sure?"

"Sure, we tried it, it didn't work out," he said.

James Kelly didn't say anything, just twisted his hands. June wanted to reach out and touch his arm, but he knew if he did, the vampire would shrug him off like he always did.

"James Kelly, you know if there's something you'd like to talk about, I'm always here to listen."

"No," he said. June made a face and that didn't sit well with the vampire, so he snapped, "There's nothing I need to say with someone like you."

"You're doing it again," June reminded gently.

James Kelly sighed. "I'm sorry."

"Do you want to just say all the nasty things at once so I won't have to be disappointed a little bit at a time?" June asked. "Just one big disappointment."

The vampire rubbed his face.

"Are thing still rough with you and your girl?"

"I don't know."

"Mmm," June said. He prepared coffees for them and set one in front of the vampire, who clasped on to it like he needed it to live. "Has someone ever done something to you?"

"What?"

"I mean...another man, has one ever made you do something? Hurt you?"

"No!"

"Cause you're very defensive about all this and if you'd been hurt, I'd understand, but I don't. If no one's hurt you...and I've never done anything, at least, I don't think I have..."

"You haven't."

"But you don't want to talk to me, it riles you up if I touch you. I don't know, it feels like there's something more to it than being uncomfortable with me sleeping with guys."

June thought the vampire would be angry, maybe even storm out on him, but instead he

put his face in his hands for a while and then said, "I don't imagine you went to high school."

"No."

"And you never had to grow up?"

"Well...I started out new, just like babies do. I had to learn."

"Alright, well, anyways, I did go to high school. I had a friend. A best friend, since we were kids. We did everything together."

"And he fancied boys, got too interested?" June guessed.

"No. Not even close. He thought I was...too interested in him. You know, cause you start to grow up and get interested in girls. Hair, zits, smells. And things get confusing, you're not sure what's what, all those changes. Anyways, we got messages crossed, somehow."

"Oh."

"And we fell out. Hard. Freshman year. And he told people."

"Ah."

"Alright, shit, June, I don't know what else to say."

"Ooo, and we're swearing? I thought your parents raised you better," June said with a smile.

James Kelly smiled, too.

"Where'd you go for vacation?"

"Maine."

"I've never been, was it nice?"

"You've never been? I thought you were old."

"Let me rephrase. I've never been to Maine as is. I saw it once before the Norwegians got there. Hung around the Penobscot for a while. Maybe twenty years. But what did you do in Maine?"

"Watched tourists eat lobster. Night time walks on the beach. Ate wild blueberries. Annie thought it was—"

"Ridiculous?"

"It's her favorite word," James Kelly admitted. "They were

good, though, it'd been so long since I'd had one. It's easier to stay on track, to be the way I want when I can be a person again. I mean, it's not that I don't like the nightlife, but I forgot how warm the sunshine is, what the grass looks like in real light. Seeing the sun on the ocean again?"

June smiled at him. "How sweet to be human."

"I'm not human."

"You're not so far off, you want to meet something really inhuman I'll find you a spriggan. Or a huldra."

"A what?"

"Fairy folk."

Gordon jumped on the table, sniffed around and settled in between the two of them. James Kelly reached out to stroke him. Gordon began to purr, rubbing his head against James Kelly's hand.

"So, um, that woman?" James Kelly asked.

"Who? Kathy?"

"Yeah, the white one with the bad hair."

"James Kelly, be nice," June scolded. "Kathy is, uh...well, I don't know. A friend I suppose. She's pregnant and needed help."

"Oh."

"Because of my nature, I have the deep need to care for things that produce life," June explained. "I used to get into cycles sometimes. Trapped in the Hanging Gardens of Babylon for decades. I've worked through it mostly, but I've been..." He searched for a word that didn't sound too whiny. "Having a bit of a rough patch. So. Kathy."

"A rough patch?"

He sipped his coffee. "Not too bad. I've been a little lonely is all, missing home and I tried to get with this guy but uh...his vampire girlfriend tried to drink my blood. I guess it rattled me."

"Oh."

"And, well, there's getting stabbed."

"You were stabbed!"

"Yeah, you brought me soup."

"Because I thought you were *sick*," he said.

"So they stabbed me to summon Kaveon, who is pretty much the last person I wanted to see right now considering."

"Considering what?"

June tightened his hand on his mug and said, "Considering he dumped me after...a-after...oh fuck, I'm ss-s-sorry," he said, choking on his words as the tears started. "Shit." He rubbed his eyes.

"June, um."

"No, it's, it's fine, I'm f-f-fine," he said, releasing his mug and burying his face his hands. He heard James Kelly moving and assumed he was running again but felt a hand on his shoulder.

"It's alright not to be fine," James Kelly said, squeezing his shoulder. He had moved his chair to sit closer to June.

"I know, it's just that he's doing so well and I'm so shit!" June said. He wanted, badly, to wrap his arms around the vampire and bury his face into his chest. He wanted anyone to be there for him, it didn't matter who. He wrapped his arms around himself, pulling in on himself, hoping it would be enough, but it didn't have to be.

James Kelly hugged him, rubbing his back, and said, "I'm really bad with crying, you know, if you keep it up you'll get me going." He tightened his arms for a minute, then let June go when his weeping had calmed mostly.

June wiped his face with his sleeve and said, "Thank you. You didn't have to."

"Crying gets to me. Always has. My mom used to tease me." The vampire handed him a napkin and said, as he moved back to the other side of the table, "Blow your nose."

June blew his nose, not really sure what to make of James Kelly's actions. He didn't know how he could go between being caring and angry with such ease.

"Was it recently?" James Kelly asked. "Getting broken up with?"

"To you, no; probably not even to me. Its just...we were together for a long time, we had something before we even officially had something. You know. We worked well together. Really well. Or I thought we did. But he left me. To be with a girl he got pregnant."

James Kelly snorted, then clasped a hand to his face and said, "Oh, I'm sorry, but you have to see the humor in that."

"It took me several years, actually," June said. "I would have been fine with it. Three of us and a little one? I'll never have my own kids. But I guess, well, they wanted it to be just two people."

"You really would have been okay with another person?"

"Sure," June said with a shrug. "I mean...it doesn't bother me. Why?"

"I don't think I could."

"I've always been partial to open relationships, though."

The vampire asked, "Open?"

"You know, you both come home at night, but it doesn't matter if you stop somewhere in between."

"You mean being unfaithful."

"It's not being unfaithful if you agree to it," June reasoned.

James Kelly crossed his arms.

"It doesn't matter to me, either way," June said, "As long as I'm with someone who loves me. That's what matters. Loving someone."

"Really?"

"Sure, a few thousand years hasn't broken me of my romantic spirit," he said proudly.

The vampire smiled at him and June smiled back. After a moment, James Kelly's smile oozed off his face and he cleared his throat. "I should probably head home, I said I wouldn't be gone long."

"Sure. Hey, do you like jazz?"

"What?"

"A friend of mine is in a jazz band. They're playing next weekend. I thought you and your girl might want to go, a double date."

"I'll ask," James Kelly said. He stood and pointed to the soup. "You probably need to heat that back up now."

"I can handle it."

"Feel better, though," James Kelly said.

"I'm working on it."

When the vampire had left, June reheated the soup on the stove, ate and then crawled back into bed to sleep for the rest of the day.

FRIDAY NIGHT, June had put on his best suit, gray flannel wool without any thin or raggy spots, though he had glanced at a pair of blue jeans. He liked the way they fit, close to his legs so that he felt like he was showing off. He thought he would look very good dressed like one of the young rebels that came to the city, in jeans and a tight shirt and a leather jacket, but the suit was more appropriate.

He picked up Peggy on the way to the jazz show. Peggy was tall, with red hair that she'd worn the same way since they'd met. He had known Peggy since aught three when she'd had him to help her establish a breeding program for angora rabbits. She sent him a sweater or scarf every Christmas; he liked to wear the sweaters when he was home alone, snuggled in a blanket and reading on the couch. Gordon liked them, too.

As soon as she walked down the steps of her townhouse she said, "June, dear, I hear you've been stabbed."

"Yes, but that was on Tuesday," he said. He had not finished recovering yet; the wound still sent shivers of pain through him and remained sore to the touch, but he was back on his feet and tired of bed rest.

"That horrible Freeman woman, I never liked her parties."

"I didn't know you'd met," he said.

"Oh, I get around," she said. "Lots of friends in lots of places. You're taking me to see a jazz band?"

"Billy's playing."

"Billy Caldwell?"

"Yes."

"I remember when he was just a little thing." She reached out and touched the scarf around his neck. "Did you wear this just for me?"

He smiled. "You know I did."

They caught up, walking arm in arm, to the bar where they were supposed to meet James Kelly and Anastasia. The other pair stood outside, waiting for them. James Kelly frowned before he waved.

"Peggy, this is Anastasia and James Kelly. New to Manhattan, James Kelly originally from Brooklyn, Anastasia from Poland."

Handshakes and greetings were exchanged and they entered together. The women went to sit at a table near the stage, one that had been reserved for them by Billy, and the men went to the bar to order drinks.

"You don't go with girls," James Kelly accused.

"I still have friends," June said, "Besides, don't make it sound like it's impossible to go with both. I don't, but you know, some people do."

The vampire ogled him for a moment, like he had said something impossible, but took his eyes from June's face to speak to the bartender, ordering a drink for himself and wine for Anastasia.

"Oh, has she given up the diet?" June asked, glancing at the wine.

"What?"

"You know," he said.

"Oh, right. Yes. For some things. She says she missed wine."

"Maybe she'll like me better for bringing wine back into her life," June said, giving the vampire a smile.

James Kelly let out a small laugh. "Maybe."

"You're doing good with your circuit?"

"I am. Really good. And I think, maybe, you're right about being able to cut back."

"Don't push yourself, we don't need any accidents."

James Kelly nodded.

When they arrived at the table and sat, Peggy said, "June, dear, let me see your scarf."

He handed it to her and she handed it to Anastasia.

"Peggy breeds Angora rabbits," June said to James Kelly.

"For what?" James Kelly asked.

"For wool."

The vampire frowned. "Oh."

"Like cashmere."

"Oh."

June's first thought was that he needed to buy something nice for him, clothe him in silk and velvet, the softest things he could buy.

Anastasia passed her lover the scarf and James Kelly said, "It's really soft."

His maker gave him a smile and touched his cheek. "You are so precious."

He rubbed his fingers over the scarf, then handed it back to June. He sipped his drink and turned his eyes towards the stage when the lights dimmed.

Peggy and Anastasia chatted with each other throughout the show and June was happy to go to the bar whenever their drinks needed refreshing. Sometimes he brought James Kelly with him and a few times, they snuck out for a smoke so as not to offend Anastasia, who hated the smell of cigarettes, standing quietly together with their cigarettes, not needing or wanting to say anything.

"Have you got a light?" James Kelly asked when he checked his box of matches to find it empty.

"Sure, no problem," June said, striking a match and holding it out.

"Thanks."

June liked to light his cigarettes for him, the vampire leaning in close to him to catch the flame from the match. The best part of June's night came when James Kelly asked to bum a smoke and June handed him the cigarette from his mouth.

The vampire took it and touched it to his own lips, without a look of disgust or any nervousness. In that moment, it didn't matter that June was gay, they were just two men smoking together, friends sharing a moment of quiet.

They went back inside and sat back down, listening to the last handful of songs. When the set finished, Billy packed up his trumpet and came down to see June and Peggy. They drank together for a little while until Peggy said, "Well, June, dear, I think I'm ready to go home. An old lady like me does need her beauty sleep."

"We should go, too," Anastasia said.

They walked out together and outside, Peggy said, "Oh, one

thing. June, you don't mind." She took the scarf from around his neck and wrapped it around James Kelly's throat. "Look at that color with your skin. Beautiful. I had to see it. What a pretty thing you have, Anastasia."

Anastasia looked at James Kelly with a smile on her face then said to Peggy, "Good night. I hope we'll see each other soon."

"We will," Peggy said.

As she and June walked home, Peggy said, "Everyone was so aflutter about you and that vampire—"

"There's nothing to be aflutter about!"

"Of course not."

"Not really everyone?"

"Everyone who knows anything," Peggy said. "That Anastasia, though, how very Old World. Maybe we can modernize her."

"It would help."

"She's stuck on murder, isn't she? Distasteful."

"You're a modern woman, Peggy, maybe you can talk her out of it."

"I can try my hardest. I do dislike murder, especially when it's so avoidable."

Back at her townhouse, June hugged her goodbye and said, "Give Marie my love."

Peggy smiled. "I will. Next time, if it's not so late, you'll have to come in and say hello. She does adore you."

At his apartment, he snuck into bed as quietly as he could, making sure he didn't wake Kathy. On Monday, she would be starting work and he'd had a firm word with her new employer, asking them to be as understanding as they could with her.

Gordon hopped off the couch and followed him into the bedroom, jumping onto the bed to wait for him to settle in. Once he had, Gordon curled on top of him and June seriously considered getting another cat. He wondered how that would affect his plants.

For the following week, June kept busy around the apartment, crafting little herb pouches and potions, teas and brews for the people he served. There was a baby in Queens with colic, three in Harlem with croup and several expecting mothers with bad morning sickness, including one who couldn't keep anything down, to the point of weakness.

He settled nicely into that routine, waking early enough to make breakfast for Kathy, then showering once she had gone. He would water his plants, trim what herbs he needed off of them and sometimes run out to Chinatown to get other ingredients he needed. By the time Kathy came home, he had run out his products and started to make dinner.

She teased him, saying that he ought to be out working and she should be making dinner, to which he always said, "Yes, Kathy, but that's very boring."

ON FRIDAY, he needed to go to Staten Island to visit a little witch at Willowbrook. He did not bother to go through the staff to get to her, knowing she would be expecting him already. He found her outside, sitting alone.

A woman in a nurse's uniform called over to him as he walked across the grounds and he ignored her. He went to sit beside the girl.

"Hello, Sissy," he said.

She glanced at him and raised one hand, her version of a wave.

Sissy, June knew, was very bright, but had been classed firmly as an idiot by the state following her mother's death, due to the fact that she didn't speak. Sissy, full name Canadensis, had been born to a single mother, also a witch. She had inherited her mother's powers and her blue eyes. At nine, her mother had died and, following several bad decisions on the part of her school and social worker, she had been placed in Willowbrook State School.

June had not been allowed to take custody of her and when he had asked to adopt her, he had been laughed at. Despite being among Satan's favored, June was not above the State of New York, so Sissy had been kept here.

"Sissy, do you know what day today is?"

She shook her head.

"June nineteenth."

She looked at him out of the corner of her eye.

"Yeah, you're right, it's your birthday. Do you remember how old you are?"

She held up her hands, showing him sets of fingers, ten and then eight more.

"Eighteen, you're so good at remembering, Sissy. Eighteen means we can go now."

She held up the doll she cradled in her lap so that he could see it. She had made, at ten, an effigy of her mother and brought it everywhere she went. June felt reasonably sure that the doll held some sort of connection to her mother's spirit.

"No, not to see Mommy," June said, "To see one of June's friends. Is that okay?"

She nodded.

"Okay, time to go." He stood and offered her his hand, which she took, then threw her arms around him. "It'll be good to visit you somewhere nice, don't you think?"

Holding hands, they began to walk out but a nurse ran over to him, standing in his way and said, "You can't—"

"Sissy's eighteen today. Every time I asked to take her out, I was told she had to be eighteen or we had to be related. Clearly, I couldn't pass for daddy. But we can leave today."

Sissy nodded emphatically.

"Sir, I don't really think you understand—"

"I've known her all her life," June said, "And I have a home for her. Please move."

"I need to talk with the director."

"That's fine, we'll wait."

Sissy screeched and he shushed her.

The nurse walked away and once she had entered the building, June tugged Sissy hand and whispered, "Run, Sis, let's go."

They booked it to his car and she climbed into the back seat; she only ever rode in the back seat. He smiled and she laughed.

"Buckle," he reminded.

She buckled herself and her doll.

June drove her out of the city and to Long Island, taking the Belt Parkway. After an hour, they arrived at the home of Paula and Bob Winston, a husband and wife in their fifties who had agreed to take in the young witch, having worked previously with people who had special needs.

He stopped his car in front of their house and got out. Sissy stayed in the back seat and he went over to her door and opened it.

"Sissy, it's time to get out now."

She shook her head.

"Yes, I want you to come meet my friends. Their names are Paula and Bob and they're witches, just like you and Mommy. They'll teach you like Mommy used to."

She pressed her lips together and then let out a high-pitched whine.

"No thank you," he said firmly.

She frowned at him.

"Come inside. If you don't like it, you can come home with me. Okay?"

She nodded.

"Unbuckle, please."

She unbuckled and grabbed her doll. She clung to June's hand as they walked up the step and he let her ring the doorbell.

A man and woman answered and smiled at them. "June! So good to see you," Bob said. They traded handshakes and Paula gave him a hug.

Sissy watched warily.

They entered the house though she hesitated at the doorstep. June talked her through it and got her to sit on the couch. Once she was on the couch, a beagle jumped up beside her and snuffled her ear.

She let out a small yelp and Bob said, "Gracie, no!"

The dog looked at him.

"No, shh, it's alright, Bob," June said.

The dog returned its attention to Sissy, licking her face and nosing her all over. Sissy grinned.

"Sissy likes animals," June said. "Sissy, do you want to stay here with Gracie?"

Sissy ignored him. He went over and crouched next to her. "Do you want to stay with Gracie and her family or go with June?" he asked. "Touch me if you want to go with me."

She shook her head and ran her hands over Gracie's ears. She smiled, giggling when the dog licked her hands.

"June, are you going to stay for dinner?" Paula asked.

"I'd love to," he said, even though dinner time was hours off.

June stayed all through the afternoon and evening, he stayed for dinner and a surprise birthday cake for Sissy. He handed over the present he had brought for her, several new dresses in colors he knew she liked.

Once she had gone to bed with Gracie draped across her legs,

June sat up with Paula and Bob discussing the girl.

"What exactly is wrong with her?" Bob asked.

June shrugged. "I think being in that place is what's wrong with her. Her mom did a lot of work with her, even got her to start talking, but when her mom died, she clammed up. I've gotten a dozen words out of her over the past couple of years...she understands fine, though, if you speak clearly. I think, with time, you two can really help her."

"We hope so," Paula said.

"Also, be careful, she hits sometimes when she's angry. I mean, not hard, we got her to stop doing that...promise you're not going to hit her back."

"No, of course not!" Paula said, "We've never used violence on a child."

He nodded. He believed them. In the years he had known then, Paula and Bob had never been anything but gentle. He'd never even seen them shout at each other or hit the dog. The couple acted as his liaison on Long Island, referring cases to him and helping the borough demons keep tabs on the creatures that had migrated out to the suburbs.

"Will she be alright when you're gone?" Paula asked.

"I told her I was going home. If she's not, you call me and I'll talk to her."

They nodded. Paula was not capable of having children and she had never asked June for help; instead, she and Bob had spent most of their lives fostering children that no one else would care for.

"She's a good girl and she's smart. She's got a lot of life ahead of her," June said.

"We're glad to have her," Bob said.

June glanced at the clock and said, "It's probably time for me to go home."

"Of course."

He stood and they stood as well. "Tell me if you have second thoughts about this. You know, I was there when she was born."

"June, don't worry."

"I'll come back to visit."

"We know."

"Call anytime," he insisted.

"We'll be alright," Paula said, putting a hand on June's arm and walking him towards the door. "Don't worry so much."

He nodded and drove home. Kathy asked him where he had been and he said, "Just taking care of a friend."

"You didn't make me dinner," she said, playfully accusing.

"There's leftovers in the fridge."

"You'll make someone a good wife someday," she teased.

He frowned, resisting the urge to ask her when she would move out. He knew she had been saving money towards it.

"What?"

"It's not funny," he said. "I'm not less because I like to take care of people or because I cry. Men should be allowed to care too and I hate all this American bullshit, crushing all your feelings down because it's how *men* should be."

"Didn't know it was such a sore spot," she said.

"Now you do."

"You've got a lot of sore spots."

"I don't like the way people treat each other," June said. "It doesn't sit right. Whatever happened to kindness?"

"Were people ever kind?" she asked.

"A long time ago. Before they were greedy." He sighed, glanced at her and said, "I'm going to bed."

She nodded.

In bed, he reflected that there were still kind people in the world, people like Bob and Paula, and even people like James Kelly, who June suspected would be very kind if he wasn't so afraid of himself.

AUGUST 3, 1953

THE PHONE rang and June grabbed it, wondering if it would be someone needing help or James Kelly inviting him out to do something. The vampire had invited him out on several of their double dates over the past few months. They had gone to museums and concerts, a few plays and the movies, with Peggy and Anastasia always whispering to each other.

"June?" came the vampire's voice, before he even had a chance to say hello.

June settled into the couch, which, although Kathy had moved in with a girl from work, was still set up as a bed; he had not gotten around to putting it back as it had been. He missed her, a little, but he did not miss all her insidious little remarks about race and gender.

"Hi, there, I was thinking of you, I saw an ad for—"

"I need help."

June sat up straight. "Why, what happened?"

"She's brought someone home, June."

"Oh, don't fret, you've been doing so well."

"June, she's *bleeding*, she cut herself, she wants me to bite her, please."

"Leave, get out."

"Come get me, please, I can't walk by her...not with the blood. Please."

"Alright. I'll be right over."

"I'm in the bathroom," James Kelly said and June imagined him leaning against the door, the whole phone dragged in with him, his knees against his chest. "No matter what I'm doing when you get here, make me stop."

"Hold tight," June said.

He didn't think James Kelly would do anything, but if it would make the vampire feel better, he would go. They could go for a walk, smoke a little, maybe get a cup of coffee and he would bring him back once Annie had finished with whatever victim she'd found.

He grabbed his coat and hurried over, slipping through the door behind someone and jogging up the stairs. He heard music coming from within the apartment that the vampires shared and quiet noises, cries of some kind. He tried the door and found it unlocked. As he entered, he still could determine if the sounds he heard were of pain or pleasure.

The first thing he saw was Anastasia, sitting in an armchair, her eyes turned towards the couch. He looked to the couch and saw James Kelly on top of a half-clothed woman, his hips between her bare legs and his mouth latched to her breast, the fabric of her blouse ripped open. He made hungry, wet noises, pressed hard against her. Blood leaked from his mouth.

June felt uncomfortable interrupting what seemed to be an odd but consensual scene, but he remembered what the vampire said and walked over.

"Get out," Anastasia warned, standing up.

"Sit down or I'll send you to see my king," he warned.

She hesitated and that gave him space enough to wrap an arm around James Kelly's waist, pulling him back from the woman. The vampire strained against him, but June held tight, pulling him towards the door.

"You asked me to come, remember that you asked me to do this," June said.

James Kelly turned to look at him. "She wants me to," he insisted.

"You don't want to," the creature reminded. "Remember what we worked for."

"Don't," Anastasia said, "I found her for you, so things will be right again. She wants it, she wants you to end her."

James Kelly stepped towards the woman. "I want more."

"Come with me," June said, "Please." The vampire hesitated and June took his face in his hands. "Look at me, you don't want to do this, think about how hard you worked."

"For what!" Anastasia demanded. "Leave, you are not welcome here."

"Shut up!" June shouted.

She flinched and James Kelly stepped out of his grip.

June grabbed his hand. "You called me, you asked me to stop you. Do you remember calling me?"

"I do..."

"You did such a good job stopping," June said, "Don't spoil it. Please."

He looked back to the woman, who lie on the couch, breathing shallowly, her eyes half-closed. He looked at Anastasia, then around the room, his eyes settling on the broken phone outside the bathroom door.

"Tell me you want don't want to kill her," June pleaded.

James Kelly's hand tightened on June's. "I don't..." He looked to the door and around the room again. "I need to go."

"Yes, let's go," June said.

"Don't you dare," Anastasia warned. "If you walk out on me, you cannot come back."

The vampire turned to look at her, pulling his hand out of June's and June felt sure that he'd lost him, that he would return to his debauched murder.

"I don't want to come back," James Kelly said, wiping his mouth with the back of his hand, leaving a smear of blood on the cuff of his shirt. "I don't want to live like this, Annie. I can't."

She screamed wordlessly and knocked over her armchair; she descended on the woman, who cried out.

June grabbed James Kelly by the arm and said, "Let's go, now."

The vampire followed after him as June led him out, stopping dead outside the door to stare up at the sky.

June could feel his heartbeat racing in the vampire's wrist. "You're alright," he said.

The vampire grabbed him, burying his face in his neck, and June flinched, thinking that he was going to be bitten, but James Kelly did nothing more than cling to him, whispering into June's neck.

"I don't want to kill anyone," he repeated.

"I know," June said, holding him tight and rubbing his back. "I know you don't."

He tried hard to think of anything but the man pressed against him, his lips moving against his throat. He was hard, not uncommon for vampires after feeding since the new blood had to go somewhere, and June tried to ignore that too, but it was difficult not to think about. He knew he should let go, step back and let the man regroup, gather his thoughts, but he didn't want to, he wanted this warm body against his.

June closed his eyes for a moment, then ran his fingers along James Kelly's cheek. The vampire looked up at him and June leaned in a little bit, not very close at all, but it was enough to make James Kelly release him and step back, shaking his head.

"No," the vampire said firmly.

"I won't," June said.

"I *don't* want you to do that."

"I won't."

"You were about to!"

"I was only going to ask," June said. "I told you I wouldn't without you letting me."

"I'm *not* letting you."

"I know!" June said. "Shit." He pulled out a pack of cigarettes and lit one, looking up at the sky and around the street, anywhere but at the vampire.

After half a minute, James Kelly asked, sounding embarrassed, "Can I get one?"

June looked at him and cracked a grin, unable to stop himself. He took out the pack and offered it to the vampire, who tugged out one cigarette, smiling too.

"And a light?" he asked, still sheepish.

June laughed at that and James Kelly laughed, too, smacking him in the arm. He grabbed June's matches but was laughing too hard to light one. June tried to help him and though it took him several tries, he managed it. James Kelly lit his cigarette and stepped back. June tossed the match on the ground.

They smoked together for a while. James Kelly glanced at him and said, "Hey, uh...I know..."

June looked at him. "What?" he asked when he'd been quiet for too long.

"I know when I feed that I get...you know. I act different."

"Happens to a lot of vampires, I'm not unfamiliar with the phenomenon," he said.

"It's still...I figure it must be hard on you..."

"Hard *and* all over me," June said, grinning.

James Kelly smacked him on the arm again. "Shut up."

"Coffee?" June asked.

The vampire nodded. "And maybe some pie."

"Blueberry?"

"I'm in the mood for apple."

They walked together to the diner and smoked while they sipped their coffee. Their usual waitress frowned at them and asked, "You two ever eat real food? Always pie and coffee."

"Hey, I always tip, don't I?" June asked.

"Figure you do," she said, leaving their slices of pie on the table and walking away.

"You should ask her out," June said to James Kelly once she had walked away.

The vampire wrinkled his nose. "Why?"

"You're single now, aren't you?"

He put his face in his hands.

"You're not going back, are you?"

James Kelly slumped.

"Tell me you aren't, not with her doing that!"

"I'm not," he said. "But after seven years...?"

"I know."

"But I'd be a fool if I said I didn't see it coming. The moment she walked in the door with that woman, I knew...I knew she would talk me into it, that I would let her."

"Have you got a place to stay? If you don't, you can crash at mine."

James Kelly said nothing for a while, clearly debating with himself.

"I don't mind the company."

"What about Kathy?"

"Kathy moved out, I told you."

"Oh. For a few days."

"As long as you need."

"Thanks."

"That's what friends are for," June said.

After they finished their pie and coffee, they went back to June's apartment. James Kelly collapsed face down onto the pullout couch. Gordon eyed him disapprovingly.

"Bed?" June asked.

"Seven years, June."

"You've got a lot more years ahead of you, don't worry."

"I thought...I don't know, I didn't ever think that there'd be an after, I just didn't think about it."

June sat on the coffee table. "You want to talk?"

"No."

"You want to drink?"

"No." He looked at the cat. "C'mere Gordon."

The cat ignored him.

"Gordon, be nice," June said, but the cat ignored him, too.

"What are all these plants for, anyways?"

"Herbs," June said. "For work. And some of them smell pretty. You sure you don't want to talk?"

"Yes. No. I don't know." He rolled over onto his back and looked up at the ceiling.

June wanted to crawl on top of him and cover him with kisses. "I know a lot of girls I can fix you up with."

"I'm not ready to get back with anyone so quick."

"Oh. That's fair. Thought you might to get laid, take your mind off things."

"No, I...I don't go for that, not right away."

June smiled. "What a nice boy, you must make your mommy and daddy so proud."

James Kelly sat up. "Just because I think you should care for someone first–!"

"I'm only teasing. Calm down. I don't judge people, not on who they want to go to bed with or how long they wait or don't wait."

"So you don't judge me for staying with Annie?"

"Staying with someone is easy, even if they're bad for you," he said. "Taking care of yourself is hard. Are we staying up?"

"Yes."

June got up and made himself a drink, just ice and whiskey. He made two, in case James Kelly changed his mind. The vampire reached out and took the drink before June could even offer it to him.

They didn't talk much during their first two drinks, mostly going around the same idea that yes, seven years was a long time and no, you can't stay with people who make you do things you don't want to do.

"More please," James Kelly said, reaching over to the coffee table and setting his empty glass on June's leg.

June got him another drink and one for himself. He brought it back and said, "Are we getting drunk?"

"Yes."

"Okay, I'll be right back," he said and returned in pajamas. He tossed a robe at James Kelly and said, "Get comfortable."

James Kelly kicked off his shoes and stripped down to his undershirt and boxers, leaving his clothes in a pile on the floor. He wrapped himself in the robe and slumped in the bed. June watched, fascinated, as he did that all with a drink in his hand without spilling a drop. One of the advantages of being vampire.

After their third drink, June brought back the whole bottle and settled onto the bed next to the vampire. "You don't mind, do you?" he asked. "I don't want to spit up...sit up anymore."

"No, you're fine," the vampire said, "You're fine. Sssfine."

"Good, I'm glad."

"What am I gonna do?"

"What'd'ya mean?"

"All my stuff...shit, I don't have...any *money*, I don't have a *job*."

"Stay here."

"No, I can't."

"Why not?"

"I don't know."

"Stay here," June insisted. He took a sip, his tumbler clicking against his teeth. "I don't want to be...I don't want, um, you alone."

"What?"

"You shouldn't be alone," June said, saying his words carefully, "You should be with a friend. With someone who cares."

The vampire blinked.

"I don't want to worry about you," June said, "I do, I worry about you sometimes."

James Kelly took a drink. "Seven years."

June laughed and looked around for an ashtray. He took out two cigarettes and shooed the cat away from his drink. "Not for cats."

He handed James Kelly a cigarette and lit it for him, then one for himself. He lay on his stomach and smoked, watching the vampire smoke. Neither of them spoke as they took drags and tapped ash into the tray. June reached out and brushed a little bit of ash off the vampire's arm, then pulled his hand back and said, "Sorry, I'm sorry."

"Sfine."

They drank a lot that night and eventually June cuddled up to the vampire, saying "I'm sorry, I'm sleepy and I don't want to get up, I'm sorry."

James Kelly reached over and patted him sloppily on the face. "I don' even care."

June closed his eyes and started awake fifteen minutes later when Gordon jumped on him. The vampire grunted and June said, "Sjust the cat."

James Kelly rolled to the side a little and said, "Okay. Gnight."

"Mhm."

June woke face down in the late morning, the cat curled up on his back. James Kelly had rolled away in the night, his face buried in the corner of the bed that touched the couch. June stretched and Gordon stood up, digging his claws into June's back.

"Ouch, Gordon."

James Kelly groaned into the couch.

June sat up, reached out and put a hand on the vampire's back. "You okay?"

"No."

"Stay, I'll make you something," he said, pushing himself up and swallowing when his world spun.

He pinched herbs from plants as he went and puttered through his cabinet until he found honey. He put water to boil and returned to the vampire a quarter hour later, warning "Careful. Hot."

"I'm going to throw up."

"Go to the bathroom!" June insisted.

"I can't move."

"If you throw up anywhere but the toilet, you're out," June warned.

"Bag."

"For fuck's sake." He grabbed a paper bag and handed it to the vampire, who put his face inside the bag, but did not throw up. He lay on his side and breathed, slowly.

June sat beside him and rubbed his back. "Come on, try to sit up, if you drink this you'll feel better."

James Kelly sat up, with a lot of groaning.

"Pathetic."

"I haven't been drunk in seven years at least."

"We'll get you used to it again."

"No."

June handed him the mug and rested a hand on his back. The vampire drank from the mug, wincing and saying, "Tastes like bad cooking."

"But does it make you feel better?" June asked, "With medicine that's what matters."

The vampire sipped a little at a time and slowly started to shift, sitting up straighter until June realized that James Kelly wanted him to remove his hand. He took it and moved so there were a few more inches between them.

"Do you want breakfast?"

"I don't need to eat."

"Yes, but do you *want* breakfast?"

"No."

June returned to the kitchen and made himself something to eat. As he cooked, the vampire slunk to the bathroom and June wondered how well they would do as roommates, even temporary ones.

ON FRIDAY night, June and James Kelly sat in the kitchen, listening to the radio and smoking with the window open. Gordon sat on the fire escape, watching the birds and chittering at them. Neither of them had said anything for a while, but there was nothing that needed to be said.

They had gone back to Anastasia's apartment and collected some of his essentials, clothes, and a few other personal items. Anastasia had watched them the whole time, playing with the hair of another young man with curls and bright green eyes. Her fingers twined in the curls, her mouth occasional pressing to his skin.

James Kelly had not been chatty since then. June didn't know what to say to make him feel better.

The door opened and they both turned to look. Wei entered with Micah behind him.

"What?" June asked.

"August seventh, you're booked, figured I'd just bring him up," Wei said.

"Booked?" James Kelly asked.

"Oh, shit, I forgot," June said.

"Alright, well, he's yours for the night," Wei said. "Have fun. Normally it's extra if someone else wants to join in, but I'll give you a pass this time."

"I don't want—" James Kelly protested.

"No, of course not," Wei said as he left, closing the door behind him.

Micah stood uncomfortably just inside the door and June got up and went over to him. "Don't worry, nothing you don't like, I promise."

James Kelly said, "And I don't want—"

"And *I* didn't even invite you," June said, "I don't care what you want." He reached up and touched the freckles all over Micah's skin. He took him by the hand and walked him towards the bedroom, then scooted back out and put his keys on the kitchen table. To the vampire, he said, "Here's my keys. Head out if you want."

"I think I will," James Kelly said, taking them up. "Is he...are you?"

"You want it blunt?" June asked, "Wei is a pimp and I'm paying Micah."

"Oh. He'll be here...all night?"

"Yes, but we won't be *busy* all night," June said, glancing at Micah, then hurrying over to him, slipping an arm around his waist and pulling him through the door, closing it behind them.

He pressed his mouth to Micah's, feeling safe. He knew that Micah would not tie him to an altar and stab him, nor would he try to distract him while someone stole his blood. Micah would be pliant and sweet, he would be grateful and generous. It was worth spending money to feel safe and to get off while he did it.

June realized that it probably wasn't healthy to form such an attachment to Micah. He rested in his arms, leaning against him and said, "What do you want to do?"

"I'm supposed to ask that."

"I want to do so many things to you," June said, listening to Micah's heart.

"June?"

"What?"

"Why do you hire me all night?" Micah asked. "I mean, I get that you want to have sex, but that doesn't take all night."

"You want to really know?"

"Sort of."

"Because I'm a sad, pathetic man and I'm so old and I just want someone to love."

"June, I, uh..."

"No, I understand that you don't want that, but you don't mind if I pretend, do you?"

"Not really, as long as you don't start following me home."

"I'm pitiful, not a stalker," June said.

"At least there's that."

"Tell me you don't want to and I'll stop calling for you."

"No, you're easy money," Micah said with a smile.

June laughed and kissed him. "Maybe I'll make you work for it tonight."

Micah returned his kiss, putting an arm around his waist and pulling him closer.

When James Kelly came home hours later, he found them in the kitchen, June in a robe and Micah in boxers and an undershirt. June sat at the table, smoking, and Micah leaned against the counter, a bowl of corn flakes in his hands.

James Kelly stopped just inside the door and June turned to look at him. Micah waved. "You're the one Wei bitches about," the human said.

June sighed. "Why's everyone talking about my business?"

"I'm your business now?" James Kelly asked, crossing his arm and frowning at June.

"Of course you're my business, you live in my borough and you tried to kill someone the first night I met you," the creature reminded.

"You're not really in charge of all the monsters around here, are you?" Micah asked.

"In charge is a very strong way to put it," June said. "I watch and listen and send in the big guns on the nasty ones."

"Like Annie?" James Kelly asked.

June looked at him. "Well...no, not unless she gets sloppy. Safeguarding human life is not my charge. If she goes too public, kills too many, starts putting the rest of us at risk, then yes, she'll be on my got-to-go list."

"Oh."

"A few years back, there was a fairy, up to mischief, as they are, but started stealing babies. And she had to go. Or there was a troll who camped out in the Holland Tunnel and started ripping tires off of cars," June said.

"A troll." James Kelly raised an eyebrow.

"Aye, son, a troll," June said. "You're a vampire, but you don't believe in trolls?"

"I don't know," the vampire said with a shrug.

"We're going to bed as soon as he finishes eating, you'll have your room back," June said.

James Kelly nodded.

"Do you like Halloween?"

"What?"

"Only a few more months, what are you going to dress as?"

"Nothing, seeing as I'm not eight."

June snorted. "Think of a costume. I'll take you out for a real Halloween, none of this candy and toilet paper nonsense."

James Kelly shrugged.

"It'll be fun. You might meet someone nice," June tempted.

"It's only been a week."

"By Halloween, it will have been months," the creature reminded.

James Kelly stifled a yawn in the crook of his arm and Micah asked, "Do you need to sleep?"

The vampire didn't answer and June cleared his throat.

"Oh, me?" James Kelly asked, looking over at Micah. "I don't know if I need to, but I get tired."

Micah nodded.

James Kelly nodded, too, and shifted uncomfortably.

"Finish your cornflakes," June told the human.

"They got soggy," Micah said.

June rolled his eyes. "Then throw them away, it's time for bed." He stood and stretched on his toes, making satisfied noises.

Micah threw away his cereal and left the bowl in the sink. June took his hand and walked towards the bedroom, saying to the vampire, "Sleep tight."

"Yeah," James Kelly said.

June closed the door behind them and snuggled into bed with the human; sleeping beside Micah was by far the most worthwhile part of paying to be with him. He wondered if he could pay for cuddling only and felt sure that somewhere in New York there was someone who would sleep beside him every night for a few dollars.

Micah left early in the morning and June handed him cab fare and stole a hug.

"I'll be broke when you get a boyfriend," Micah teased.

June smiled. As he walked back to his bedroom, he noticed that James Kelly was awake but pretending not to be. "Hey," he said and saw the vampire move a little bit, his eyes scrunching closed a little more. "Come on."

James Kelly said nothing.

June reached over and picked up Gordon off the pullout bed

to cradle him in his arms. "At least you always come home," he said to the cat and went into his room to lie in bed for a few more hours.

He didn't get out of bed until he heard James Kelly moving around the apartment. He found the vampire in the kitchen with a bottle of whiskey in his hand and he said, "Uh, bit early?"

"You left it out."

"Oh. I probably did."

James Kelly returned the bottle to the cabinet it belonged in.

"You want breakfast?"

"No."

"Kathy always wanted breakfast." June pouted for a moment and the vampire gave him a nasty look.

"Sorry I'm not some girl you can fawn over," he said.

"You're always so grumpy," June said under his breath, walking towards the fridge in a straight line so that the vampire would have to move, that or run the risk of having June brush up against him.

As expected, James Kelly moved aside and June took the milk out of the fridge and closed the door harder than needed. It should not have bothered him that James Kelly didn't want to be touched by him, but it did. He brooded over it as he ate his Kix and realized that it was not that James Kelly didn't want to be touched, it was that he was allowed to touch June and June was not allowed to touch him.

June had grown used to humans touching him over the years; they liked to touch his horns and children liked to climb in his lap. Women often rested their heads on his arm and men would put their hands on his shoulder. He didn't think it had to do with fertility, but with the fact that his body and consciousness had been made by a god. He had been touched by the divine and even though he had fallen from grace, he was the closest most humans ever got.

He put his bowl in the sink when he finished, beside Micah's, and after he showered, he decided that he would call Kathy later in the day to see if she needed anything.

Once dressed, he gathered the things he needed to deliver that day and on his way out, he said to James Kelly, "Spare key's in the junk drawer. There's a bunch of job applications in there too. You might want to look at them."

The vampire looked up from petting the cat with a nonplused expression on his face. "Oh."

June nodded and left, wondering for the rest of the day if he had been too unkind. He came home in the evening, saw that James Kelly had gone out, and called Kathy, sitting on the coffee table with Gordon in his lap and both of them playing with the phone cord.

"You ever talk to the father?" he asked.

"I rang him and he's seeing someone else. I didn't bother to tell him."

"Mhm," he hummed sympathetically. "How's the job?"

"Not so bad. I hardly make any typos anymore."

"That's good. How're you feeling?"

"Not so bad yet."

"The tea helps with your stomach?"

"Yes. Thanks."

He heard the door unlocking and said, "Give me a call if you needed anything."

"I will."

"I've got to go."

"Bye."

He hung up, replaced the phone, straightened the blanket where Gordon had mussed them and wondered what was taking the vampire so long to open the door. He went over and turned the knob, pulling the door open and saw James Kelly with blood dribbling down his chin and tears on his cheeks.

He almost fell over when June pulled the door open.

"Are you fucking kidding!" June said, "What did you do now!" He grabbed the vampire hard on the arm, knowing his claws would be digging into his skin and maybe even making him bleed, pulling him inside. "Coming back to my home fucking looking like that!"

He pushed James Kelly through the door and was ready to keep shouting when he saw that he didn't look like he had been feeding, he looked like he'd gotten the shit kicked out of him.

"What happened?" June asked, ice lancing through him.

"I don't know."

"What do you mean you don't know?"

"All these people came and-and-and they grabbed me and they...they..." He continued, but June couldn't understand him.

"People or creatures?" June asked, wondering if this could have been racially motivated.

"I don't know," he said and buried his face in his hands.

June took him by the arm, much more gently this time, and led him to the bathroom. He ran water until it was warm and wet a washcloth. He pulled the vampire's hands from his face and said, "Here, let me see."

James Kelly shook his head, still crying.

"You're a mess, come on," June said. He noticed that the spit coming from his mouth was tinged with blood and said, "Let me look at your mouth." He put the washcloth in the sink, turning off the water.

Asking to see his mouth made James Kelly cry harder and he put his face back in his hands, hunching over on himself. June closed the toilet seat and had him sit on it, handing him a box of tissues; he sat on the edge of the bathtub, not knowing what he was allowed to do to provide comfort.

Enough humans could get a jump on a vampire, or even just a few skilled ones. It was entirely possible that maybe James Kelly had wandered somewhere where black men were not welcome though the vampire seemed very aware of where he was allowed to be.

June reached out and put a light hand on his back, wondering if this would make things worse. The vampire did not flinch and June rubbed his back for several minutes until he calmed. June took the washcloth back up and dabbed at the blood on his face, holding his chin softly, careful not to scratch him any more than he had dragging him through the door.

"I'm sorry I shouted, I thought you had been killing people."

The vampire shook his head.

June wiped around his mouth and he jerked back, startling June. "I'm sorry," June said. "Let me look at your mouth."

He shook his head.

"Did they hit you in the mouth? You shouldn't be bleeding so much, especially being what you are."

"They made me...they opened my mouth and—" His breath caught and he clenched his hands. "They put this *thing* in my mouth to hold it open...and..."

"Let me see," June said, suspecting he knew what had happened, coldness spreading through his body.

James Kelly barely parted his lips, but June could see that his fangs had been ripped from his jaw, not gently or cleanly, leaving his gums ragged, with cuts all over his gums and tongue, with some on his lips.

"Did it seem like they were looking for you?" June asked.

The vampire nodded.

"Alright," he said and pressed the washcloth into his hand.

"Wash up, I'll get you some clothes and some ice."

James Kelly nodded.

June found a pair of comfortable looking pajamas for him and wrapped some ice in a few towels. He held out both and James Kelly took them, but only held onto them.

"Do you want help?"

The vampire nodded and June thought that he must have been really rattled to want him to help. Once he was washed and changed, June had him hold the ice to his mouth and walked him to his bed. The vampire held on to the ice as though it were his only connection to the world and June sat beside him on the bed, settling him in and pulling up his covers.

"Poor thing."

"They knew my name, June. They were waiting for me on my way home."

"I'm very sure I know what happened," June said, reaching over to adjust some of his wayward curls and to pick debris out of them.

"What?"

"It's a vampire thing, a punishment. For traitors."

"I haven't done anything to anyone."

"Anastasia might think otherwise."

"She wouldn't..."

"I think she did. Unless you've been pissing other people off. If you were rough on one of your donors, it could be a vamp gang."

"No, I'm always careful!"

"I'll look into it."

"You're not going to hurt her!"

"No, not yet."

"June."

"I'm going to make some calls and see if I can't find out who put a hit on your chompers."

"It really hurts."

"It's supposed to," June said. "Your mouth will be healed up in a few days and the fangs will grow back."

"They will?"

June nodded. He fixed a few more curls without thinking and then pulled his hand back, tucking it under his leg. He started to chew on the claws on his other hand.

"My stomach hurts."

"Did you get hit in the stomach?"

"I got hit all over," he said.

"Poor thing," June said and really meant it.

Looking pathetic, James Kelly asked, "Will you turn on the radio for me?"

June smiled. "Of course, I will." He got up and switched on the radio, already tuned to the station James Kelly liked. He went back to sit on the edge of the bed, not sure if he was allowed. "You should get some rest."

"Are you doing anything for the rest of the night? I mean, you don't have plans, do you?"

"No. Why?"

"I just...I don't want to be alone."

"Don't worry, you won't be."

"Uh."

"What?" June asked.

"Nothing."

"Alright. I've got a couple things to brew up, let me know if you need anything."

James Kelly nodded.

June went to the kitchen and took a pair of scissors, clipping what he needed from his plants. He spent the better part of two hours in the kitchen and one more at the kitchen table spooning everything into jars and bottles. He stashed them in the fridge, then went back to the living room.

"I'm done for the night. You all set?"

James Kelly nodded.

June changed into pajamas and brushed his teeth. On his way back from the bathroom to the bedroom, James Kelly made a sound that nearly sounded like a word. June paused and asked, "You need something?"

"Uh."

"What?"

"I really don't want to be alone."

June titled his head. "But do you need something?"

"Can you stay?"

"Out here?"

James Kelly nodded, not able to look him in the face.

"Sure," June said, coming over to the couch.

"I'm sorry," James Kelly said.

"For what?" June asked. "I know you're shook up." He pulled back the covers and cozied in, nestling his face into the pillow.

James Kelly looked at him and June realized the vampire had not expected this. "I don't know where else you'd want me to sleep, or did you just expect me to sit on the coffee table all night?"

"I'm sorry," the vampire said again.

"Go to sleep," June said and closed his eyes.

In the morning, June awoke to see that Gordon had curled between them during the night. James Kelly still slept and June took a few minutes to look at him, running his fingers along the cat's spine while he looked.

The cat swatted his hand away after a minute and he cried, "Ouch, Gordon!"

James Kelly's eyes opened and June sat up. The vampire blinked a few times, rubbed his eyes and asked, "June?"

"What?"

"You don't really think Annie did this, do you?"

"I'm going to find out."

"I don't want to know."

"Are you kidding?"

"Please, June, I really don't want to know."

"Fine. How's your mouth feel?"

"Not so bad."

"And the rest of you?"

James Kelly sat up and shrugged.

June reached over and patted his shoulder. "Don't worry, you'll be okay."

The vampire sighed. June wanted to hug him and he looked like he needed to be hugged, so the creature took a chance and leaned over to wrap his arms around the vampire. James Kelly leaned against him without flinching or going rigid, returning the embrace the way a frightened child might hug their parent.

"Thank you."

"You're welcome."

"I put in a lot of those applications yesterday."

"I didn't mean it, I was being mean."

James Kelly pulled back, his brow knitted. "Why?"

June shrugged. "I don't know."

"Oh."

"I'm going to go take a shower," the creature said, pushing back the covers and heading for the bathroom. He cleaned up and dressed, then paused to look at James Kelly, who still lay in bed with the covers pulled up.

"Are you going to be alright while I'm out?" June asked.

The vampire nodded.

"Do you want to come with me?" he asked, wondering if James Kelly still worried about being on his own. "I don't mind the company."

James Kelly hesitated a long time, his eyes moving uneasily, his lips almost forming words until he said, "I could. If you wanted company."

"I do. Get ready, I'll wait," he said.

He puttered around the kitchen as he waited, checking his plants and to see if Gordon had enough food and water; he made a grocery list and finally sat at the table, chewing on one of his claws until James Kelly emerged from the bathroom dressed and ready to go.

He didn't talk much while June did his errands and June didn't push him. When they returned, James Kelly went back to bed but didn't sleep, lying awake with his covers pulled all the way up to his chin.

AUGUST 23, 1953

AFTER LOSING his fangs, James Kelly did not venture out much on his own and June worried about him. He went to feed and always looked nearly sick on his way out the door. Some nights he skipped his feedings all together and as the night ticked by on what would have been his third skipped session, June said, "I'll walk you over before it's too late."

James Kelly looked up at him from his seat at the kitchen table. He had been staring into the dregs of his coffee for near to fifteen minutes.

"You need to take care of yourself," the creature said as he trimmed some of the languishing stems from a parsley plant.

"I'm just...I'm not in the mood."

"A vampire not in the mood for blood?" June asked.

"You said that some of us only go once a week."

"I did," June admitted, "But I didn't ever think you'd be one of them."

The vampire frowned and said, "Besides, I haven't got a lot of money left."

June put down his scissors and asked, "James Kelly, are you hungry or not? Don't go starving yourself to save a couple bucks."

"I don't have a job, I need to save."

"No one's called?"

"They were all jobs looking for a girl, anyways, shop girl, maid, waitress, secretary...No one wants me for that kind of stuff."

"You didn't put in anywhere else?" June asked.

The vampire looked down at his hands.

"Not that I'm telling you do!" he said, "But you've mentioned it a couple times."

"I...I don't want to have to...after what happened, walking alone...I don't know," the vampire said, still not looking at June.

June came over to sit beside him. "I'm worried about you."

"Don't be."

"But *I am*," he said, "It's in my nature to want things to thrive and you are not thriving."

"Sorry," James Kelly snapped.

June didn't know what else to say; he wanted so badly to take care of this man, who clearly needed someone to care for him at this time. His affection had never been rejected in such a confusing way before and he didn't know what to do. He stood and went back to his parsley, clipping off the yellowed leaves.

If he looked back at the vampire, he would cry, he knew he would and he almost started crying anyways. It was stupid; James Kelly had done nothing but reject him.

Except for the time he had hugged June to soothe his crying, or the times when he had nuzzled against him after feeding. Except, there were the times June caught him looking at him and the way they smiled at each other sometimes. Except for the way he asked June to stay up with him until he fell asleep because, since the attack, he'd been afraid to be alone. There were so many things he did that were not rejection, that were more than simple friendship.

The phone rang and June rushed to grab it. "Hello?"

"June!" came a voice on the other end, the voice of a girl or a young woman, and it took him a long moment to place who it could be.

"Sissy?" he asked.

"Hi, June!"

"Hi, Sissy," he said, "It's so good to hear from you. Is there something you needed?"

"Just say hi," she said. "Paula's turn."

"Hi, June," said Paula.

"Hi. She sounds good."

"She is good, June, she's so good. You should see her and Gracie. She wanted to say hi, I told her she could call after she did her work."

"Is she doing a good job?"

"We're doing really well with reading," Paula said.

"Can I talk to her again? Say goodbye?"

"Of course; here she is."

"Sissy? You there?"

"Yes," said the girl.

"Paula says you're doing a good job. I'm so proud of you. I'll come see you soon, okay?"

"Okay."

June smiled. "I'll talk to you later. Call me whenever you want."

"Okay. Bye, June," she said and he heard the phone hang up.

He hung up his end. He felt peaceful for a moment and reveled in it, closing his eyes and letting himself smiling. The feeling didn't last long. He sighed and went back to trimming his plants; more than the parsley needed looking after and he wondered if he could look after plants too much.

He ran his fingers along a lavender blossom and wished that plants could love. Of course, he knew a few beings who argued that plants could love and that they loved better than things made of flesh, but they were mostly fairies and June didn't trust them.

"You've got a sister?" James Kelly asked.

June turned around, his brow furrowed. "What? No," he said, "Well, I mean, I have lots of sisters, but not like humans have sisters."

"So who were you talking to?"

"A girl I know," he said, "Someone I've been looking out for."

"You do that, don't you?" James Kelly asked.

"What?"

"Look out for people," he said.

"Suppose so," June said.

"Like me."

June shrugged and turned back to his plants. He didn't want to talk to James Kelly, not right now, not while he had his eyes trained on June's face in a thankful, sad way.

"What's that about?" James Kelly asked.

"I don't have anything to say," June said. "Sorry."

"You always have something to say."

June turned back around and gave him a nasty look, then turned back to his plants. He wandered around the apartment for another hour, trimming and watering and adding soil to some of his pots. He noted which ones needed to be repotted and jotted down how many pots he needed. He would run out later, or maybe tomorrow, to get them.

"Are you mad at me?" James Kelly asked and June stopped dead at the way he asked, hesitant and careful.

He turned around. "Why would I be mad at you?"

"It feels like you're mad at me."

"What does it feel like when someone's mad at you?" June asked, rolling his eyes and turning away again.

"It makes my stomach hurt."

He turned back around, not liking that answer at all, and thought that if he kept turning back and forth, he would throw up. "I'm not mad at you."

"So why do you keep playing with your plants instead of talking to me?" the vampire asked.

"Because you don't want to hear what I want to say to you," June said.

"What's that mean?"

June shook his head.

"You can't just say things like that," James Kelly said. "Tell me what you meant."

June wished he hadn't said anything. His face grew hot as he tried to think of a way out of what he had started.

"June."

June ran a hand through his hair. "I mean...don't you feel it?"

"What?"

"Between us."

"I told you—"

"I know you did! That's why I didn't want to talk about it," June said. "But sometimes...the way you look at me, it doesn't *feel* like we're just friends. It feels like something more. And I know you've told me off a dozen times, but I don't understand how I can feel something that isn't there."

"Oh."

"Right. Oh."

James Kelly stared at him.

"It's not just me, I've...I've noticed you looking at other men," June said.

"I don't."

"But if you do, it's alright," June insisted. "I don't care if you don't want to be with me, but I do care if you're hurting yourself.

It's no good for you to ignore part of yourself."

"I'm *not*."

June sighed and said, "I'm going out."

"Why?"

"Because I don't know how else to end this conversation, but it's not my place to tell you who you are. Make sure you let Gordon back in when he comes to the window," June said, looking around for his keys. He grabbed them and headed for the door.

He didn't know where to go, so he sat on the stoop and smoked for a long time, going through the rest of his pack because he didn't want to go back inside. He walked to the store and bought another one, but didn't start it.

He took the long way home and when he arrived, found James Kelly sitting on the stoop, his own pile of cigarette butts beside him. June stopped in front of him and rubbed the back of his neck, not sure what to say.

James Kelly looked up at him and took a drag on his cigarette, then stubbed it out. "June, I...I really don't know what to say. I'm sorry, I don't."

June sat next to him.

"I mean...I'm dead. I've been dead for seven years and I've spent that time killing people with a woman I thought I would be with forever. I don't know how I feel about a lot of things because I thought I wouldn't have to think about it anymore, not as long as I had Annie with me."

June started to open his new pack of cigarettes.

"But..."

"But you don't and that's fucking you up. I get it," June said, putting a cigarette in his mouth and lighting it. "All I'm saying is that you should let yourself feel what you're feeling. That's it."

James Kelly took June's pack of cigarettes without asking and pulled one out. He returned the pack and held out his hand; June knew he was waiting for matches and he handed them over.

"I don't want you to think that I'm saying all this because I'm trying to get something out of you," June said.

"I know," the vampire said and stayed quiet for a minute after that. He ran his hand through his hair and glanced at June, then added, "I really do. I know I'm not fair to you. If you wanted to do something to me, you could have done it by now."

June didn't know what to say, so he nodded.

"Besides," James Kelly said out of nowhere after several silent minutes had passed, "I wouldn't deserve to be with someone nice anyways. That was the good thing about being with Annie, we were both killers."

June snorted. "I've been living on this earth for millennia, you think I haven't taken a life? You killed people for seven years, I did it for fifty."

"What?"

"Georgia. Not the best time in my life, I got...caught up in something I shouldn't have," June said. "I don't like to talk about it, but don't go thinking that I'm some harmless idiot with too many plants. Maybe I started out innocent but that didn't last."

The vampire shifted.

"You deserve what everyone deserves."

"What's that?"

"To be with someone who you care about, who cares about you, and neither of you makes each other do things you don't want to do." June sighed and stubbed out his cigarette. "Did you let Gordon in?"

The vampire blanched. "I forgot," he whispered.

"Don't worry, I'm going to go check on him," he said. He patted James Kelly on the shoulder, stood and headed inside.

"June?"

He paused and looked back.

"You're a good friend, a great one...but friends is all I'm ready for. With anyone."

"That's fine," June said and went inside. He let Gordon in and turned on the radio so he could listen to something other than his own thoughts as he tried to get to sleep. He heard James Kelly come in a while later; he turned off the radio and June could hear him trying to be quiet as he got ready for bed.

SEPTEMBER 8, 1953

AROUND FOUR in the morning, June woke up, sitting straight up in bed, his heart hammering. Something had crashed in the living room and he scrambled to get out of bed to find out what had happened. He extended his claws without thinking and went forward, ready for the worst. He found the door smashed open and James Kelly climbing over the coffee table to get away from the men who poured in.

June counted three men pushing their way through the door, all vampires and all white. James Kelly grabbed on to his arm and said to June, "That's them."

"You're sure."

"The smell," he said, "I know the smell."

June wasn't sure what these men could be here for, not when last time they had taken James Kelly's fangs and those hadn't grown back in all the way yet.

"Hand him over," one of the intruders said, coming closer. As he edged closer, June caught a whiff of Brylcreem and a combination of colognes, English Leather and Pinaud Clubman. These vampires reeked, not just of too much cologne but of rotten flesh and swamp dirt.

Judging by the smell, they were part of Brana's gang, who ran out of an abandoned factory in Mariner's Marsh, where they ritually nested with their victims after the weeks-long process of holding them captive and draining them.

They were not much loved by most, but they were discreet and good for dirty work, so they were tolerated.

"You've already taken his fangs, what else could you want with him?" June asked.

"None of your business," the vampire answered.

"He's one of Manhattan's creatures and that makes him my business," June said, "Same as living on Staten Island makes you Nico's business."

The man stopped advancing, which June was glad for since his smell was making June's eyes water.

"Manhattan's lucky to have a nice fellow like me in charge, but Nico's not so nice, I know he runs a tight ship over there. Here you come breaking into the home of one of his colleagues?"

"We've got a contract to fill."

"Break it," June advised.

The vampires all looked at James Kelly and their leader said, "If you knew what he'd done, you wouldn't defend him so quickly."

June let out a bark of laughter. "Coming from the leeches who kidnap prostitutes and bums and bed down with their corpses? What could he have done?"

The gang vampires bristled at his comment and he'd known they would. "He's a traitor."

"I gathered from the way you harvested his teeth. What did he *do*?" June demanded, knowing that there were certain rights James Kelly could invoke.

"He betrayed his maker, one of the high crimes."

James Kelly's grip on June's arm tightened. June grabbed his hand and said, "Contest her accusation."

"What?"

"Say 'I contest her accusation'," June said.

"I contest her accusation?" James Kelly said.

The vampires surged forward and grabbed James Kelly, who pulled back. June grabbed him and said, "No, we have to go now. Don't worry, I'm coming with you. And the rest of you, hands off." He smacked the other vampires' hands away from James Kelly. "We haven't even got any shoes on. Get your shoes."

June pulled on his shoes and couldn't tie them, then realized he hadn't pulled his claws back.

"One of you go get Anastasia," June said once they'd put on their shoes and were all standing around.

"Go," the leader said to one of the gang vampires.

The leader then grabbed James Kelly and June smacked his hand away again. "Hands *off*," June said, "This is my borough, I don't know how you do things in Staten Island."

"He could run," the leader insisted.

"I won't," James Kelly whispered.

"I'm vouching for him."

"Where are we going?" James Kelly asked as he and June were herded out the door.

June made sure he had his keys, then answered, "The Apthorp. It's where Louisa and Michael live."

"Who are they?"

"Your monarchs."

"What?"

"I mean, for vampires, not for the United States, obviously."

"I didn't know we *had* monarchs."

"Antiquated, I know, a lot of people are calling for it to end, but until they do, it's up to them whether or not Anastasia is justified in claiming betrayal," June said.

"Is she?" James Kelly asked.

"Of course not."

"That's not for you to say," another vampire snapped.

"No, but I think I'll have some input," June said.

James Kelly held on to June's sleeve for the whole walk. By the time they arrived at the Asthorp, June wished he'd had time to at least brush his teeth. Once inside, they were brought to a parlor and waited. June sat and James Kelly began to pace.

The two remaining vampires from the gang stood in the doorway as though they had been appointed guards.

June reached out and took James Kelly's hand; the vampire stopped and looked at him and June said, "Sit down, please."

James Kelly sat and continued to hold on to June's hand, running a thumb over one of June's nails over and over again.

"You'll be alright," June assured. "They're not stupid and I have sway with them."

"You said you didn't have pull with the vampire gangs."

"The gangs, no, but Louisa and Michael have a relationship with my king, delicate as it is," June said, "They'll take my word seriously."

The vampire's hand tightened on his and June would have given anything to make him feel better, but his new fangs were barely poking through his gums and he still hesitated to go outside alone. Being accosted in the middle of the night was not what he needed.

June heard people entering and Anastasia entered the parlor. She took a seat on the other side of the room and didn't look at them.

After her arrival, they waited for about ten more minutes until a vampire, who must have been twelve or thirteen when she was changed, came into the room.

"Their Majesties will see you now," she said and turned around, expecting them to follow.

June stood, still holding James Kelly's hand, and followed her into a spacious and elegantly decorated room. Furniture had been moved to the sides of the room to make space for a line of chairs that faced two thrones that were little more than chairs themselves. June only knew them as thrones by the crests that decorated them and the two vampires who stood beside them: Michael, his head shaved and his eyes sightless, and Louisa, a woman with skin the color of teak.

"Sit please," said the vampire child.

June and James Kelly sat on one end and Anastasia sat as far from them as she could, still not looking at them.

Louisa looked down at the note in her hand and said, "James Kelly Rosenburg, please rise."

James Kelly stood.

"You are accused of betraying your maker, which is considered to be a grave thing among our kind. How long have you been vampire?"

"Seven years."

"And the woman here, you can confirm that this is your maker?"

He looked at Anastasia. "Yes, she is."

"And the man you've brought with you, is he to serve as a witness or...?"

"Uh, yes?" James Kelly said.

"Sit."

James Kelly sat.

Louisa turned her eyes to June and said, "Please rise and state your name and any titles you might have."

"Junius Thompson, malak ha-satan, among the first fallen," he said, "Watcher of Manhattan in service to He Himself, the prince of darkness and lord of hell, who sits upon the serpent's throne." He added after a moment, "His wife calls him Luci." He smiled to himself.

"And your relationship to the vampire on trial?"

"Friends."

Anastasia made a sound of disgust, louder than it needed to be.

"Quiet, please, unless being addressed," said Michael without looking at Anastasia. He asked June, "Is there anything you'd want to add?"

"Good friends, I supposed. Roommates. They broke into my apartment to get to him."

Michael nodded. "You may sit."

June sat.

"Anastasia? We have no last name on record for you, but it hardly matters," Louisa said. "Rise and state your case against your fledgling."

Anastasia stood. "He has betrayed me, betrayed my trust and care, taken all that I have given him and taught him and thrown it away. He has shamed our ways, our traditions. He left me for this...horned creature before you."

"I—!" James Kelly cried out.

"Shh," June said, putting a hand on James Kelly's arm, "You'll have your turn. No calling out, didn't you learn anything in school?"

He saw Michael smile.

"Can you give any examples?" Louisa asked.

"I have stated the things he has done."

"I must warn you," Michael said, "That is not a very compelling case. Surely, we are all disappointed when a relationship comes to an end, no matter the circumstances, but that is not a high crime."

"No," Louisa said. "How has he shamed our traditions?"

"He refuses to take blood the correct way."

"Hmm," Louisa said. "You may sit."

Anastasia sat but crossed her arms.

"James, you may rise."

He stood and said, "It's, uh, it's James Kelly."

"Noted," Louisa said. "This is your chance to defend yourself."

With a small shake in his voice and a nervous cadence, the vampire said, "I can't say I know that much about vampire tradition, I don't know if I've done anything wrong...but I do know that Annie and I started to have problems when I, well, when I decided to stop killing folks to drink from them. June, um, he set me up with a circuit of donors instead."

"This ended your relationship?" Michael asked.

"Annie wasn't happy that I wanted to change and...um. She tried to get me to keep killing. She managed to once. The second time, I walked out."

"Anastasia, is this the betrayal you speak of or is there something more?" Michael asked.

Anastasia pressed her lips together and nodded.

"Much easier," Michael said. "I hope we can avoid each other in the future. James Kelly, you are free to go, Anastasia, if you put another contract on him, we will send you to meet Junius' king. Give our regards, if you see him, Junius."

"I will."

"We're so sorry you had to come all the way out here for such a little thing."

"There is the matter of my apartment door," June said.

"Of course, we'll send someone over. Still at the same address?"

June nodded. "I am, thank you."

"You're free to go," Luisa said.

June stood and tapped James Kelly on the arm. The vampire rose and they exited in silence. They returned home in silence and June propped the front door closed with a chair, kicking the debris to one side.

He sighed and looked at the mess their little scuffle had caused, chewing on one of his claws. He glanced over at James Kelly, who stood on the far side of the room next to the coffee table, and asked, "Are you alright on the couch tonight?"

James Kelly shrugged, his eyes on the floor. June walked over and took his hand, not knowing if he'd be rejected, but the vampire grasped his hand. June walked into his room with James Kelly shuffling behind him; they lay down together and James Kelly curled up on his side facing away from June, pulling his covers up.

June gave him his space, knowing he wanted it, but he reached out and touched the vampire's back. "Let me know if you need anything."

"I'm okay. Thanks, though."

June rubbed his back once and then took his hand back, tucking it close to his chest, burying his face in his pillow.

James Kelly returned to his own bed the following night since the door had been repaired. Once he'd gotten into bed and as June headed towards his own bedroom, the vampire called, "Do you think she'll stop?"

June paused. "Hmm?"

"Annie, do you think she'll really leave me alone now?"

"I hope so," June said and thought that if she didn't leave him alone, it would be the last thing she did. That thought was too protective and harsh to share aloud, though, so he kept it to himself.

James Kelly nodded.

"Sleep tight," June said and went to bed.

An hour later, someone knocked on his bedroom door and he thought about getting out of bed, but called, "What?"

"I can't sleep," came James Kelly's voice through the door.

"Come in."

The vampire entered.

June pushed himself up and gestured for James Kelly to come sit beside him. "What do you want?"

James Kelly came over and shrugged. "I can't sleep is all."

"You want me to tire you out?" June asked, giving the vampire his best smile.

James Kelly hesitated and June reached out to grab his hand. He tugged the vampire towards his bed and while he didn't come eagerly, he didn't resist.

James Kelly said, "Don't say things like that."

"I'm sorry. Do you want to listen to the radio or something? I've been thinking about getting a television," June said. "Do you like to go to the movies?"

"I do. Annie hated them."

"Tomorrow I'm going to take you to the movies."

James Kelly shook his head. "Tomorrow I have to go to Brooklyn."

"Oh. All day?"

"Yes. But maybe we can go a different day."

June settled back against the pillows and asked, "What kind of movies do you like?"

James Kelly shrugged.

"I like Marlon Brando. I went to see *Julius Caesar* with Peggy this summer. You know, based on the play?"

"Sure."

"Have you seen *A Streetcar Named Desire?*" June asked. "I'm a Tennessee Williams fan, I have to say."

"He's a writer?"

"Hell of a writer," June said. He sat up and looked around his room, saw what he searched for and got up. He took a few books off his shelf and handed them to James Kelly. "Highly recommended."

James Kelly looked at them, then set them aside.

"I mean it, save them for next time you can't sleep," June said.

"I'll read them."

June made a face.

"I will!"

June grinned. "I believe you. Are you sleepy yet?"

"No."

"I hear warm milk is supposed to help, I don't know how it does for vampires. We could mix in a little blood, make it go down easier."

James Kelly wrinkled his nose and turned down his mouth, his face contorted into pure disgust. June grinned.

"So are you going to keep me up all night?" June asked.

"I'm sorry."

"Do you have a lot of sleepless nights?"

"No," he answered, then thought and amended, "I didn't think of them as sleepless, anyways, Annie and I would stay up and talk if one of us couldn't sleep."

"What do you want to talk about?"

"I never had a dog. I always wanted one," James Kelly said. "My cousins on Long Island had a dog. She died when I was twelve, but I always liked her."

"I've had dogs," June said, "In between at the moment, as you can tell, I don't think Gordon would like a dog very much. I've been thinking about getting another cat. There are so many little lost animals that need homes."

James Kelly nodded. "My grandmother has a lot of cats."

"Do you like rabbits?"

"Never met one."

"Lavender."

"What?" James Kelly asked, turning to face June.

"Lavender, that will put you to sleep."

"You don't like talking to me, do you?"

"I like talking to you a lot, James Kelly, but it's past my

bedtime. Stop that fake pouting, it's going to work on me."

"Don't you mean it isn't going to work?"

June shook his head. "No, I mean it's definitely going to work," he said, smiling at the vampire.

James Kelly cleared his throat. "Uh. I'm going to go read," he said, taking the books from before. "Good night."

"Stop by anytime."

The vampire walked out without saying anything else.

In the morning, he left before June woke up. June tended his plants for a little, ran some errands and talked to Gordon, until an idea struck him and he called Peggy.

James Kelly came home late and June asked, "What in Brooklyn could have taken all day?"

"Oh, no, I stopped on the way home to drink."

June nodded. "No plans tomorrow?"

"No."

"Good," June said, "We're going to see a movie."

James Kelly nodded. "That sounds fine."

"Did you do any reading last night?"

"Um, a little."

"Did you like it?" June asked.

James Kelly shrugged and leaned down to pet Gordon, who had come over to wind around his ankles. "Hello, did you miss me?" he asked the cat.

Gordon meowed.

"Is it okay if I pick him up?" the vampire asked.

"Um, it doesn't matter to me," June said. "I don't think Gordon minds either."

James Kelly picked up the cat and cradled him to his chest. Gordon didn't seem to mind either; he put a paw on James Kelly's chest and looked up at him. "You know, I never had any pets growing up. I always wanted one."

"You mentioned last night. Your parents didn't like pets?" June asked.

"No, I, uh, I had allergies. Cats and dogs. And peanuts."

"Really?"

"I guess, being dead gets rid of allergies, though," James Kelly said. "I don't need glasses anymore either."

"You had glasses!"

James Kelly looked up from cooing at the cat and nodded. "Yes. Since I was eight."

"I bet you looked good in glasses."

"No one looks good in glasses."

"I bet you did, I can imagine it. A wee little thing with your curls and your little smile!" June said, grinning at him.

James Kelly shook his head and set the cat down on the back of the couch. "I didn't have curly hair when I was young either. Well, I mean, it was curly, but my parents kept it short."

"Doesn't change your smile, though," June said.

The vampire rolled his eyes. After a moment's thought, he touched his hair. "It still grows."

"What?"

"When I died, I didn't think it would grow anymore, but it does."

"Well, you're only mostly dead," June said, "And you've got all sorts of magic making you tick."

"Only mostly dead," James Kelly repeated with a touch of dryness in his voice.

"Much better than all the way dead," June reminded, "You've never met a zombie. They rot."

"Ugh."

June came over to the couch and stroked Gordon's head. "I've been thinking about getting another cat."

"You mentioned."

"I was telling Gordon."

The vampire scowled, but it wasn't a serious scowl, it was almost a smile and June felt very proud of himself. "What movie are we going to see?"

"It's a surprise," June said and gave no answer other than that.

THE FOLLOWING evening, they stood outside Peggy's house and James Kelly said, "This isn't a movie theater."

June didn't answer but went up and knocked on the door. A woman with pale purple skin answered and he said, "Marie!"

"June! Peggy said you were coming by, I can't tell you how excited I was to hear," she said.

James Kelly eyed the woman from the bottom of the stoop.

"Come in, please," Marie said, "And your friend too. Is this the vampire I've heard about?"

"Shh, Marie, no gossiping," June said.

James Kelly followed June inside and when Marie left to find Peggy, he asked, "Is she one of you?"

"What?"

"She's purple."

"Oh, no, she's not fallen. Lots of people come in lots of colors," June said.

"What is she?" the vampire asked.

"What are you?" Marie asked with an edge her in voice, coming back with Peggy on her heels. Peggy had an absurdly fluffy rabbit in her arms.

James Kelly glanced at June, looking uncomfortable. "Don't answer," June mouthed to the vampire.

"Peggy, you didn't tell me Ginger was going to have babies," June said, reaching out to take the rabbit.

"She isn't," Peggy said.

"Oh, she is," June said.

Peggy looked at Marie with her lips pressed together.

Marie shrugged. "Sometimes they want to play together."

Peggy sighed.

June held out the rabbit to James Kelly and he reached out with a hesitant hand to touch the animal.

"So, what are you?" Marie asked, training black eyes on the vampire's face.

The vampire hesitated. "Uh."

"Marie, don't be rude, please," Peggy said. "Marie has inherited some bad manners from her father."

"At least I don't go around asking what people are," Marie said under her breath.

"Fairies, all the same," Peggy said with a smile.

Marie clucked her tongue. "Anyways, everything's set up in the living room," she said and walked away.

Peggy gestured for them to follow and walked after Marie.

"What are we doing in the living room?" James Kelly asked.

"I said I was taking you to see a movie," June said.

"Oh."

"Come on, it'll be fun," June said, cradling Ginger in one arm and reaching out to take the vampire's hand with the other.

James Kelly pulled his hand back but followed the others into the living room anyways. They had a screen and projector set up. "Peggy has a copy of *A Streetcar Named Desire*. Aren't we lucky?"

"I am a woman of many means," Peggy said, taking the rabbit back from June and handing it to James Kelly.

"No, that's okay—" he began.

"You've been staring at her," she said, putting the rabbit in his arms. "Ginger likes movies too."

Marie seated herself on the couch, nestling into a corner.

"Have a seat," Peggy said.

James Kelly took the other corner with Ginger on his lap and June sat next to him. Peggy turned off the lights and turned on the projector and speakers, checking a few things, then sitting in between June and Marie. Marie immediately pulled her legs up and put them on Peggy's lap, who did not bat an eye.

"Let me know if you need anything, I can make drinks," Peggy offered.

"No, we're fine," June said.

"Let me know," she said firmly.

June nodded and reached over to give Ginger a pat on the head; James Kelly did not flinch and June felt surprised, realizing that he had expected the vampire to flinch.

"June?" James Kelly asked quietly after twenty minutes.

"What?"

"She makes sweaters out of these rabbits?" he whispered.

"Yes."

"How...how does she get the fur?" His voice came, worried and soft, through the darkness.

June turned to look at him. "A pair of scissors, silly, don't worry. Just like sheep."

"Oh."

"Do you know how they shear sheep?" June asked.

"Shh," Marie said.

"Shh, you," June said, glancing at her.

"I don't."

"Poor city mouse," June said, "We'll take you to the country."

"Shut up," James Kelly snapped.

June didn't push his buttons any more than that, at least not on purpose, though he had a hard time shutting up during the movie. He leaned in several times to point out favorite scenes and to tell James Kelly to pay extra attention to certain parts.

"Junius Thompson, I don't care who your king is, if you don't stop talking, I will hex you into silence for a thousand years," Marie hissed, leaning across Peggy to do so.

"Marie," Peggy scolded.

"I mean it," Marie said, leaning back into her corner with her arms crossed.

Halfway through the movie, Ginger wriggled out of James Kelly's arms and Peggy picked her up, saying, "She must be done with us. I'll be right back."

She took the rabbit and returned a few minutes later, taking back her spot between June and Marie, shooing Marie's outstretched legs out of her way.

Without the rabbit in his arms, James Kelly tensed up considerably for the rest of the film, his hands folding in his lap and his arms pressed close to his sides. June tried to move over towards Peggy as much as he could without squishing her. By the time Blanche was being carted away to an asylum, he'd ended up with Marie's feet on his lap.

The film ended and as Peggy got up to deal with the projector,

June scooted further from the vampire. He could feel James Kelly relax once they had more space between them.

June said, "You know in the play Alan—"

"Had an affair with a man?" Marie said. "We know."

"Sorry, I think it matters," June said. "Peggy, you've got *Arsenic and Old Lace*, haven't you?"

"I do."

"I've seen it," James Kelly said. "It takes place in Brooklyn, I had to go."

"In forty-four?" June asked, doing the math in his head.

"After. Annie got a copy."

June nodded.

"Who's Annie?" Marie asked.

James Kelly opened his mouth a little, then shrugged and said, "A girl I used to go with, I guess."

"You guess?" Marie asked.

"Leave it," June advised.

The fairy crossed her arms again.

"You don't like it when people ask you about Lina," Peggy reminded.

Marie frowned immediately.

"Do you want to stay for a drink?" Peggy offered.

June looked at James Kelly before answering. The vampire said, "I'm alright, thank you, though. Unless you want to?"

"No, I'm fine," June said. "I mean...I wouldn't mind a cup of coffee or something, but..."

"We can stay," James Kelly said.

"No, I don't want—"

"Coffee it is, then," Peggy said. "The kitchen is this way, there's room for all of us."

She walked away and they followed her, with Marie bringing up the rear. They sat around the kitchen table and once they had coffee before them, June asked, "Did you like the movie?"

"Hmm?" James Kelly asked, looking up from his coffee, which he had been stirring, waiting for it to cool a little more.

"You didn't say if you liked it or not," June said.

"Oh, I did," the vampire said.

"June makes us watch it at least once a year," Marie said to James Kelly, who looked at him.

"It's only been out since fifty-one," June argued, his face feeling hot.

"So we saw it in fifty-one and fifty-two and now we've seen it in fifty-three," Marie said, "And we've been to see it on Broadway. Twice."

"Don't go just blaming June, I like the film as well," Peggy said.

"See?" June said, feeling a little better.

"I saw Kaveon the other day in the Otherworld," Marie said after several minutes had ticked by quietly.

"Marie, you're really being rude, now," Peggy said.

Marie continued unbothered, "He and Liz were with that changeling of theirs, something about a sore throat."

June frowned. "What?"

"You didn't hear? About a hundred years ago, someone took their little monster baby, the little girl, switched it out. Your king came around the Otherworld all stomping and raging to get it back. Of course, now they've got the changeling with the rest of their spawn."

"I don't know if you should call them spawn," June suggested.

"What else do you call the offspring of a demon and a werewolf?" Marie asked. "Spawn."

"A werewolf?" James Kelly asked.

June nodded.

"I mean, but don't they die?" the vampire asked. "Annie said they did, that they don't get a long life like we do."

"Oh, they do," June said, "Unless you go making deals with the Devil to keep your girlfriend around."

"He can do that?"

"He's Satan, he can do whatever we think he can," June said.

The vampire frowned but sipped his coffee instead of asking any more questions.

"I didn't even know they had more than one kid," he said to Peggy.

"Three. And the changeling," she said.

"Ugh."

She patted his back.

"Still not—"

"Marie," Peggy said. "What's gotten into you?"

"Nothing," Marie said. "Just in a mood, I guess."

"I figure we should go," June said, standing up.

"June, you don't have to," Peggy said.

"No, I'm tired, anyways, thanks for having us," he said, giving both the women a hug goodbye.

James Kelly waved to both of them and once they were outside, asked, "I set her off, didn't I? Asking what she was?"

"Probably. She's sensitive. Half human, half fairy, not at home with anyone," June said.

"I get that," James Kelly said.

"Not a lot of people in the synagogue quite as dark as you?" June asked with a half-smile.

"No, not very many," he said.

"You must not have been very good in Hebrew school."

"Why not?" James Kelly asked, offended.

"When I introduced myself to you, I told you what I was. Malak ha-satan. But you still asked who my king was."

"Maybe I just wanted to be sure," James Kelly said. "Can I get a light?" he asked, putting a cigarette in his mouth.

June handed him a book of matches.

"Anyways, sorry she took it out on you."

"She didn't mean anything by it, not really. Marie's a good friend."

James Kelly nodded, lit his cigarette and shook out the match, tossing it onto the sidewalk. He made sure it was out by grinding it into the ground with his toe. He handed back the book and said, "Thanks."

"How come you've never got your own?" June asked.

"Annie always carried a lighter in her bag. She always used to carry the keys, too," the vampire said. "I guess I have to get used to being on my own."

"I wasn't saying I mind."

"I shouldn't depend on you," he said firmly.

June almost bit his tongue, but didn't manage it; he said, "You can if you want; you can depend on me as much as you want."

The vampire took a nervous, quick drag on his cigarette and started coughing half way through.

"Sorry," June said.

James Kelly shook his head. "I don't know what you want from me, June."

June looked up at the sky and asked, "You want the truth?"

"I don't think so. I can't...I can't give you anything."

"I'm not asking for anything," June promised.

"I..." he said, then shook his head.

"What?"

James Kelly said, "Nothing."

"Please?"

The vampire sighed. "I don't think...I think I'm...I don't know, I feel like you're waiting for something from me and that it's holding you back from meeting someone else."

"No."

"June—"

"I was single before we met, nothing's changed except that I made a friend," June said and wondered if it counted as a lie. It didn't feel entirely true or false. "A directionless, unemployed friend who sleeps on my pullout couch."

"I can leave."

"I know you can," June said, "But it's you or get another cat and I really get the feeling that Gordon wouldn't get on well with a new cat. He fights with that tom in the alley all the time and I don't need the two of them tearing around knocking over all my plants."

"It's just...I feel like I'm...I don't know, always taking, not giving anything back."

"So give something back, if you're worried. Water the plants, feed the cat. Bring in the mail," June said, then added, "Do the litter box! God, that would make up for a lot of taking."

James Kelly smiled, but it looked like he was trying not to.

"Come on, pick up the pace, I'm ready to go to bed and I think Gordon was out when we left."

"No, he came back in," James Kelly said.

"See, there you are, giving back and letting the cat in."

"I can't tell if you're being mean or not."

"I'm very nice, James Kelly, I'm surprised you'd think I'm being mean," June said.

The vampire sighed and shook his head; he didn't talk to June for the rest of the night, not unless the mumble he gave in response to June's 'sleep tight' counted.

OCTOBER 19, 1953

"COME HERE," June called from the kitchen, where he had been for several hours.

"Why?" James Kelly asked.

"Just come here," June said.

The vampire appeared in the kitchen with the *Times* crossword and a pen and June beckoned him over to the kitchen table, which he had covered with silk and ribbons.

"What are you doing?" James Kelly asked.

"Halloween is coming up."

"Oh."

June stood with a tape measure in hand and stepped towards James Kelly, who stepped back.

"For fuck's sake, stay still, I'm not doing anything to you." He wrapped the tape measure around the vampire's head in a few places and jotted down the numbers. "You can go. Don't touch that."

James Kelly pulled his hand back from the completed mask on the table, made of black silk and covered with silver embroidery. "You need a mask for Halloween?"

"For the party we're going to, yes," June said.

"You made that?"

"Sure."

"It's really good."

"Thanks."

"I mean, it's beautiful," James Kelly said.

June looked at his mask. "You've never been to court if you think that's anything to shake a stick at. You should see the gowns of Eleanor the First. *That's* embroidery. Her wedding gown!"

"You're making that one for me?"

"Are you going to make your own?" June asked.

"I guess not."

June grabbed the vampire's hand and held out a swatch of champagne colored silk next to his skin, then held it up next to his eyes. He nodded and sat back down. He arranged some of the things on the kitchen table and looked back up at James Kelly for a moment.

"What?"

"Nothing."

"June."

"You're just...*really* good-looking," June said. "I mean, you're up there, kid."

James Kelly laughed. "Nothing compared to Marlon Brando."

"You blow him out of the water," June said. "All of them, any of those film stars."

The vampire frowned.

"What, didn't anyone ever tell you?" June asked. "Anastasia called you handsome, I heard her."

He shrugged. "She did, but I don't know, I guess I thought it was because she loved me. You know, all that in the eye of the beholder."

June looked up at him, waiting for him to continue, feeling that he had more to say.

"I was a funny looking kid, I guess, it's hard to think I grew out of it. And no one in the movies really looks like me, unless it's one of those African safari movies or a bellhop. And, you know, Uncle Remus."

"What about birthin' babies?" June asked.

James Kelly smiled.

"Good thing she turned you, though," June said, "Now the world can see your face forever."

"Um, anyways, do you need help?"

"Do you know how to sew?" June asked, turning his eyes away from the silk on which he'd started to trace an outline.

"No."

"Then no, I don't need help, thanks for asking, though."

"Okay." The vampire headed back towards the living room.

"You know what?"

James Kelly glanced back.

"Can you actually take that bag right there on the chair?" June asked.

James Kelly pointed to a paper bag.

"Yeah, can you take that to 5F?"

The vampire picked it up and peered inside. "Sure, what is it?"

"Just something Lizzie Berman asked for," June said. "If she tries to give you money, don't take it. Don't let her parents see you, either."

"Alright, I'll be back," he said and left with the bag in hand.

He returned a quarter of an hour later with a few crumpled bills clutched in his hand. He held the money out to June and said, "She started crying and made me take it."

June shook his head, took the money and put it into his rainy day fund on top of the fridge. He peered inside and saw that he had accumulated a decent amount; now all he needed to do was think of what to use it for.

"What did I bring her?" James Kelly asked.

"Lizzie has a shitty dad and an idiot boyfriend," June said as he sat back down, "Last thing she needs is a baby before she's even done with high school."

The vampire tilted his head in thought then said, "Oh."

June shrugged.

"Isn't that kind of...I don't know, the opposite of what you do?" he asked.

"No."

"Oh." James Kelly stood in the kitchen for a little while longer and finally asked, "Why not?"

June looked up and, with a smile, explained, "Immature, unprepared mothers with no means of their own? That's not best for anyone."

"Suppose."

"Go listen to the radio or something instead of standing around. Finish your crossword puzzle."

He walked out shaking his head and June bent back over his mask, wondering if he had stashed away enough money to buy a television, something he had been considering for a while. After a little while, someone knocked on his door and he ignored it, sure that James Kelly would get it.

As he threaded a needle he heard Douglas Berman ask, "Where's that monster who lives here?"

"Uh...June?" James Kelly asked and the demon recognized it as a call for help more than asking Doug Berman for clarification.

June set his things down and hurried out to the living room, going to the door and putting himself between Doug and the vampire. "What?"

The man, white with a jaundiced look about him, held up the bag that James Kelly had dropped off. "Saw your houseboy give this to my daughter."

"Sure, what of it?" June asked.

"Well, what the fuck is it?" Berman demanded. "I know what kind of shit you deal in, filthy sex stuff!"

"Ho, calm down," June said, "Fertility, not sex. I mean, sure, they kind of go together but—"

Berman grabbed him by the shirt and pulled him closer. "What did you give my daughter? If I find out you—"

"Stop," June said, "And let me go before I put one of your eyes out." He wrapped his hand around Berman's wrist, extending his claws and pressing the points into the inside of his wrist.

Berman hesitated and June pressed harder.

"I know a lot of less friendly demons who traffic in less friendly trades," he reminded.

Berman released him. "What did you give her?"

"Herbs."

"Don't be smart! For what?"

"For her period," June said. "She gets cramps."

The man stared. "What?"

"You know, that thing that happens once a month to people with uteruses," June said, "They bleed and all that."

He wrinkled his nose.

"So she gets cramps, I gave her something to help," he said. "I'd give them back, I hear cramps are terrible."

"What are you doing talking to her about that sort of thing?"

June frowned. "I talk to lots of people about lots of things."

Berman crumpled the bag and tossed it at June's feet. "Stay away from my family," he said and stomped away.

June picked up the bag and sighed, wondering what he how he could get them to her now. He closed the door and went back to the kitchen table, sat for a moment and found that the want to sew had gone. "Fuck."

"I'm sorry, I thought no one saw me," James Kelly said from the doorway between the kitchen and the living room.

June shrugged. "Sometimes things go wrong. Nothing to do about it."

"June—"

"Don't you have a crossword puzzle to finish?" June asked.

James Kelly stared at him briefly then walked away. They didn't speak for the rest of the evening and both of them spent a lot of time going outside just to get out of the apartment.

A few mornings later, June woke up not naturally as he did most mornings, but because he'd been jabbed in the side. He looked up to see the vampire standing over him, already dressed and smelling like soap. June looked at the clock and saw that it was just past six.

"What?"

"Where'd you put that bag? The one for the girl?"

"Why?"

"She left for school, I want to catch up with her."

"Uh, it's uh, in the fridge, I think."

James Kelly nodded and walked away. June lay back down, not awake at all, and tried to go back to sleep. He lay with his eyes closed for a while, hearing the vampire root around then leave. He heard him come back and he came into June's room.

"I gave it to her," James Kelly said.

"Okay."

"I thought you'd care."

"Too early," June said and pulled his covers up higher. He rolled over and pushed his face into the pillow.

The vampire came over and smacked him. "You're welcome!"

"Ouch!" June said, rolling over and sitting up. "What was that for?"

"I fixed it," James Kelly insisted, "I did something wrong and I fixed it. You can't be upset with me anymore."

June squeezed his eyes shut for a moment, ran his hand through his hair and said, "I'm not upset with you."

"You are, you've barely said anything to me since."

June stared up at him, not fully awake and trying to think of what he should say. "I, uh, sorry? I'm not upset. Why are you dressed already?"

"And go after her in my pajamas? Bad enough that she's a

white girl in high school," James Kelly said.

June nodded. "It's too early, you should go back to bed."

"I'm already up."

"I *know* you're already up, I said you should go back to bed," June said.

"I can't," he said and walked away.

June lay in bed for about ten more minutes, then gave up on going back to sleep and went out to the living room. He found James Kelly on his bed with a book and sat next to him. "You really thought I was upset about Lizzie's dad?"

"Yes."

"Why didn't you say anything?"

"Because I apologized and you told me to go away."

"I didn't, well, I didn't say it exactly."

The vampire shot him a look. "It's what you meant."

June waited a moment and said, "I wasn't talking to you because I thought you were mad at me again. Thought you were being broody since you weren't talking to me. I didn't realize you were sore 'cause I'd snapped at you."

"What?"

"I figured I'd done something to bug you, smiled at you the wrong way or said the wrong thing or tried to touch you too much," June said. "So I thought, let him fume, I haven't done anything."

James Kelly looked at him for a second, then looked away. "Oh," he said, his voice sort of strangled.

"What?"

He shook his head. "Nothing," he said.

"You sure?"

The vampire swallowed and stole another glance. "I don't like that I made you think there's a wrong way to smile at me."

"Well, there is, isn't there?" June asked. "You always tell me off if you think I'm being flirty."

"But a smile?"

June shrugged. "I don't know. What are you reading?"

James Kelly showed him the cover. "*The Martian Chronicles*."

"Any good?"

"Yes."

The demon nodded. He sat for a while and after a few minutes, thought he should get up, leave the vampire alone, but just before he started to stand, James Kelly asked, "Um, about this Halloween party?"

"Yeah?"

"Are you, um, are you bringing someone?"

"You mean like a date?"

The vampire nodded.

"No. Why?"

"I don't know, you haven't been...going around with anyone, not even that fellow who you paid."

"Are you asking if my love life is okay?"

"I guess. I don't know, having me camped on your couch can't be helping anything."

"I, uh...never mind."

"What?"

"I like having you around," June admitted, "You're good company. You talk back to me when I talk to you."

"Gordon doesn't talk back to you?" James Kelly asked, struggling to keep a smile off his face.

"No, does he talk back to you? That bastard, I knew he'd been holding out," he said with a grin. "What about you? Am I allowed to ask about your love life?"

"I...you know, I don't have anything to say."

"I think you should ask Avery out."

"Who?"

"The waitress!"

"Oh. No," James Kelly said. "I couldn't."

"Why not?"

"Because I don't know what I want," he said. "I really don't."

June nodded, not knowing what to tell him. "Coffee?" he asked.

The vampire nodded. "Thanks."

"Breakfast?"

"No."

"One of these days I'll get you to eat."

"I don't *need* to eat," James Kelly insisted.

"I know, but I make good oatmeal, you should try it," June said. "I finished your mask, by the way, you have to try it on and make sure it's alright."

OCTOBER 31, 1953

JAMES KELLY had been fussing with his tie for ten minutes before June went over to him and straightened it out. He did it, fighting with his desire to do it gently and the vampire's insistence that they would only ever be friends, then stepped back and handed him his mask. "Are you ready now?"

"I can't wear that out."

"Sure you can, it's Halloween. I'm wearing mine."

"I don't know, June."

June took back the mask, put a hand on the vampire's shoulder and spun him around. "Don't move," he said and placed the mask over the vampire's eyes, tying it snugly. "Let me see."

James Kelly turned to face him and June reached out to straighten it a little, unable to keep a smile from his face. The mask had come out nicely and looked even better on his face, the champagne of the silk made lovelier by the brown of his skin and eyes. June wanted to tell him that he had beautiful skin; it was not the deep, near-to-black brown of original man, but its color was rich and warm.

"All set. Let's go," June said.

James Kelly reached up to touch his mask and June pulled his hand away from his face, saying "Don't fuss with it."

James Kelly didn't yank his hand back, allowing June to grasp it lightly until he had to let go to open the door and lock it on the way out.

"Is anyone I know going to be there?" the vampire asked as they walked.

"Probably everyone," June said, "All the creatures in Manhattan anyways. It's an important party."

"Why?"

"It's like Christmas," June said, then glanced at James Kelly, "Uh, well..."

"Is there going to be a tree, then? Are we supposed to have gifts?" James Kelly asked. "With a big fat man in a red suit?"

"No, I meant that it's a big deal, that everyone looks forward to it. It's when we catch up with people."

"Oh."

"I didn't mean...I mean, I just forgot."

"It's fine."

Neither of them said anything until James Kelly abruptly asked, "Do you celebrate Christmas? I mean, considering...?"

"Not religiously," June said, "But if there's someone who wants me around for a holiday, I won't object. I like celebrations."

"But you believe in all that? The Christian stuff about Jesus?"

"Mmm, that's tricky. Worship, definitely not. Believe? I don't know. By the time Christ was around, I wasn't privy to Heaven's plans anymore. So I don't know what he was. More than human, certainly, and a nice enough guy from what I've been told."

"Oh."

"Don't sound so disappointed. Did you think I knew everything?"

"No," James Kelly said but it sounded like a lie.

June smiled at him and reached over. "You've got something in your hair," he lied and pretended to pick something from his curls.

"Thanks."

They arrived at Hotel Elysée about an hour after the party was supposed to have started and found themselves exactly on time. June hesitated before he entered the foyer, recalling what had happened the last time he had gone to a party here.

"Something wrong?" James Kelly asked, his eyebrows knitted a little.

"Uh, no, thought I'd forgot my keys," he said and forced himself inside, reminding himself that it was unlikely anyone would try to hurt him tonight.

"You look upset."

June shrugged. "No, just...might run into some people I don't want to see, I guess."

James Kelly nodded. "I've sort of worried about that, too," he admitted.

Once they entered the room the creatures had rented, someone immediately called out to him, a little boy, eight years old, with a pretty green mask on. "June!" the child cried, wrapping his arms around him.

"Andrew! Hello, you've gotten tall."

The boy grinned up at him, showing missing teeth.

"Where's your father?"

"Over getting drinks," he said, pointing to Wei, who stood in front of a table, picking up glasses. "Daddy!" the boy shouted.

Wei turned and shrugged, without a free arm to wave with.

"Go help your father," June said, giving the child a push. He walked over, too, taking the drinks out of Wei's hand and saying, "Where's your wife?" He scanned the crowd but didn't spot her.

"I can carry them," Wei insisted.

"Oh, and did you get sight back in your eye, too?" June asked.

Wei frowned.

June handed Andrew a glass and said, "Carry this for your father."

The boy held it very carefully and walked at a crawl towards his mother. June loaded up his hands and James Kelly's and followed after him.

He handed a glass to Wei's wife and to his daughter, who was in her late teens, June was sure. He kept held out his hand to James Kelly and the vampire handed him a glass.

"Thank you, dear, you're so thoughtful," June said as he took the glass.

The vampire frowned and June couldn't be sure if he was confused or irritated.

He looked at the champagne saucer and said, "You know, it's always champagne, you'd think they'd try something else."

"It's free," Wei reminded.

"Who pays for all this?" James Kelly asked.

"We don't know," June said.

"I'm sure *someone* here knows," Wei said, "But not us."

"Oh."

"Don't complain," Wei advised. "Do you want t'have a seat?"

"I think I should make the rounds, see who else is here."

Wei nodded. "We'll be here. Or chasing this one around," he said and gestured to Andrew.

The little boy grinned. Wei patted his head and June smiled at them.

"Come on," he said to James Kelly, "Or do you want to have a seat? I can mingle alone."

"No, I, uh, I'll come with you," James Kelly said and followed as June walked away. Softly, he confided, "Wei always tries to get me to hire someone."

"He's got girls, too."

"That's not what bothers me."

"Right, I forgot," he said, waving a hand at him.

"Forgot what?" James Kelly asked tersely.

June glanced at him. "That you don't do casual. Do you get offended by everything or just the things I say to you?"

The vampire frowned.

"Just me then, I'll assume," June said.

"No!" he insisted.

"Mm, anyways, I can see Peggy and Marie," June said and walked towards them; they were standing before a table covered with snacks. "Who the fuck put out a crudité at this? It's Halloween, not Thanksgiving."

"There's bruschetta, too," Marie said. "Deviled eggs, too, do you like those or is that someone else?"

"Someone else," June said. He took a plate and picked over the food put out, filling it with a half a dozen different things. He took a piece of gravlax and held it out to James Kelly. "Gravlax," he said.

"No, thanks."

"You can get your own plate if you don't want to eat mine."

"I'm not hungry."

"Usually, they have a bunch of people...yes, there they are," he said, "The ones all in white with the red masks. They hired donors." He pointed.

James Kelly looked to the person he had pointed to and said, "It's rude to point."

"Jesus," Marie said.

"Shh," Peggy said. "Do you want to come sit with us?"

"I don't know, I'm kind of wandering."

"Well, I'd avoid that part of the room," Marie advised, pointing to a far corner, "Unless you want to see Kavcon's beautiful little family."

"He never comes to these!" June said. "For fuck's sake."

"I thought you were over him," Peggy said.

"So did I, but I hadn't seen him in three hundred years and now...I don't know," June said, rubbing his neck.

"You'll be fine, it's not like he's single," Peggy assured.

"No, there is that," June said. "I'll check back in later. Do you want to stay with them?" he asked James Kelly.

"I want to leave," he whispered.

"We just got here!" June said, turning to look at him and seeing that he'd gone grayish. "What's wrong? Do you not feel well?" He reached out to touch him and he stepped back.

"I just want to go," he said.

"Alright, fine," June said.

"Just give me your keys, you don't have to come."

"No, I'll walk you out, at least, I'm sort of worried," June said, putting his hand on James Kelly's shoulder and walking with him.

"Not this way."

"The door's right there," June insisted and pushed him forward.

The vampire dug in his heels and turned around, grabbing June hard by the shoulders. "There has to be another way out."

"Sure, alright, calm down," June urged, taking him by the hand and pulling him towards the back of the room, towards the door that the wait staff used.

"June, hey—" someone called.

"Sorry, Manny, I'll be right back," he called back and kept walking, pushing through people and keeping a hold on the vampire, whose hand had gotten cold and sweaty.

As he walked, he felt a hand grab his sleeve and he looked over and had to pause when he saw who had found him.

"June!" the young witch said and smiled at him.

"Oh, Sissy, hi, I didn't think you'd be here," he said, smiling at her.

"We know you come every year," Bob said, "We thought you'd like the surprise."

Sissy hugged him and said, "Surprise."

"It's a good surprise," he said, returning the hug. "But I have to go."

"No!" she said.

"I'll be right back, I promise, I just need to do something."

"No," she said, holding on to him tighter.

He stepped back, pushing her away by the shoulders. "Sissy, my friend doesn't feel good, I have to take him out."

Sissy looked at James Kelly and slapped him on the chest; June grabbed her hands and said firmly, "No, that's not okay. No hitting." He released her and she went for the vampire again; June snatched her hands and said, "*No!* No hitting. If you hit, you will leave."

"June *stay*," she insisted with tears in her eyes.

June looked at James Kelly, who was looking at the exit desperately.

"Sissy, June will come see you, we'll go sit," Bob said, taking Sissy by the hand.

"I will, I promise," June said. "First go sit, then I'll come see you."

Tears continued to leak down her cheeks, but she walked away with Bob and Paula towards a table. June noted where it was and turned to James Kelly. "Let's go."

"It's too late," James Kelly said, staring into the crowd. "She's seen me."

"What?" June asked, looking where the vampire looked. "Oh."

Anastasia had spotted James Kelly and came through the crowd, two handsome and well-built young white men trailing behind her.

"You can still run," June murmured.

"Shh," James Kelly hissed.

Anastasia came up to him and said, "I didn't think you'd be here."

"I, uh...I am."

"I can see that," she said, "Still, I'm surprised. I didn't think you had the stomach to be around real creatures."

"We were, uh, heading out," June said, reaching over to take James Kelly's hand.

James Kelly pulled away from him. "No."

"You look sick," she said, "I suppose all that...*clean* living isn't agreeing with you."

"I'm fine."

"You always were weaker than the others I've turned," she said, "Maybe you were born that way. I never did believe in mixing blood."

"Hey," June said, "If you're just going to be nasty!"

"And a Jew, too, you think you'd be at least clever," she said.

"But you've got the worst of both, stupid like a nigger, feeble like a kyke."

"That's enough," June said, stepping between her and James Kelly. "You've got no business saying things like that to him."

"Pathetic," she said.

June grabbed her by the arm and pulled her close. "He's better than you and—"

"Stop it, June," James Kelly said. "I don't need you sticking up for me."

He released the woman. "You can't let her say things like that."

"And should I manhandle her, too, so she can say that I'm a brute?" James Kelly asked. "Let her throw slurs around, I'm used to it."

"Used to it!" June said. "You let her say things like that?"

"Her and the rest of the world! What am I supposed to do?" the vampire said.

"He knows how to be docile," Anastasia said, "It's what he's made for. He listened well before you got your claws into him."

June took a deep breath and said nothing.

"Maybe I should have let you crawl away when I saw you trying to escape; seeing you has left a bad taste in his mouth," she said. "I must have been especially tender-hearted when I shared my blood with you."

"Stop!" June said, "He's stronger than you are, strong enough to care about others more than taking a life."

"I *don't* want you to stick up for me," James Kelly said.

"Someone should," June said.

"Not you," the vampire said.

"Oh, right, not me," June said, "I forgot. Anyone but me, anyone but a *fag*. Who knows what I could do to you? I might even *care*."

"Stop," the vampire said, his voice clipped and quiet.

Anastasia laughed. "I'm not even surprised; being a faggot would explain so much of your weakness. And lack of skill."

"I'm not!" James Kelly insisted.

"Oh, she can't call you a faggot, but she can call you anything else she likes!" June said. "Because what would happen if you were, why would that be so bad!"

"Shut up," he said.

"What would happen if you were?" June asked again, his throat feeling tight as he looked at the vampire. "It wouldn't be bad."

"Stop!" James Kelly yanked the mask off his face, tossed it on the floor and walked away, not looking back even once as he left through the servant's entrance. June watched him go, not knowing what else to do. Flight was not the response he had wanted.

He had a very clear of idea of what he had hoped would happen; it had been stupid and romantic, but it had been better that the vampire had walked away. It made things very clear.

Anastasia laughed again and put a hand on June's shoulder. She leaned in close and said, "He'll never love you, you know. No matter how much you want him to, there's no such thing for people like you. In all your long life, you've never been worth keeping to anyone."

He turned around.

"I have been asking around about you, a little bit," she said, "I wanted to know something about the creature who took my pet from me. Junius Thompson, always the pursuer, never the pursued, always the one being left behind, never doing the leaving."

"I don't need this," he said and turned away again, not knowing where he would go.

"And the last one left you for a woman. Not surprising, it *is* the natural way of things," she said.

He grabbed her by the throat, nothing but anger going through him; it had been years since he had gotten this angry, maybe not since Georgia. Fifty years' worth of compelled fights had done enough to quell any urge to fight for years. There were words he could have used, but he didn't want to use them.

He felt his fingers dig into her throat and break through the skin, puncturing the pipes and arteries; he felt it before he realized what he was doing.

Filled with cold panic, he yanked his hand back, making the wound worse. Anastasia dropped to the floor, her hands scrabbling at her throat as blood gushed over them. It was a wound even a vampire couldn't bear, not with that much blood being lost. The two men who had come with her stared, one covering his mouth and the other turning away after a moment.

"Fuck, shit," he said. He dropped to his knees and closed his eyes and started to pray, as hard as he could, begging for help.

Not half a minute had passed before he felt a hand on his back. The room filled up with excited whispers and calls. "Give me a little space to work, Junius," came a soft voice.

June scrambled back. "Please, fix it."

"Shh, of course," said the Devil.

He reached over and put his hands over Anastasia's throat, then drew them back, showing the flesh that was whole and smooth again, though still smeared with blood. Satan wiped his hands on the skirt of her dress.

She lay still for a moment and one of the men knelt beside her, touching her neck.

"She'll be fine," the Devil said. "Junius, we need to talk. This isn't like you."

June threw his arms around the Devil, pressing his face into his chest. "I shouldn't have," he said.

"Oh, your hand, it's all dirty," the Devil murmured.

"I'm sorry," he said and began to cry. "I'm so sorry."

"Shh, now, it's alright, I fixed it, don't worry," he said, running his fingers through June's hair.

"You can't fix it," he cried into his king's chest.

"I think we need to take you home, yes?" he said, standing with his arm around June.

"No, I told Sissy I would go see her."

"She'll understand."

"She won't."

"Fine, but you're a sight, really," his king said.

June rubbed his eyes with his clean hand and put the other one in his pocket. He went over to the table where Sissy sat and said, "Um."

"June?" she asked, looking up at him, frowning.

"I'm sorry, I think I've got to go home."

"Sad."

"Yes," he said, "I am. I want to go home. Can I come see you a different day?"

She looked up at him for a while, then nodded her head and said, "Yes."

"Give me a call, we'll talk about it."

She nodded again and said, "Bye, June."

"Bye, Sissy."

Satan took his hand and walked him out, ignoring the others who tries to get his attention. "Still in the same apartment?" he asked.

"Yes."

His king brought him home and helped him clean up. He glanced at the neatly made bed in the living room and said nothing;

he pet the cat and put June to sleep.

"I do have to go soon," he said, "But will you tell me what's got you ripping people's throats out? It's not like you at all."

"No," June whispered into the pillow he clutched.

Satan sat beside him on the bed. "Can I look?" he asked.

"Yes."

The Devil pressed a hand to June's chest and closed his eyes; after a few minutes, he pulled back and said, "Oh, Junius, you always did have a tender heart."

"Tender enough to maim someone."

"Shh, she'll think twice before she tries to hurt someone again," the Devil said. "About *your* vampire—"

"I don't want to hear it. He's not mine, he'll never be mine."

Satan lay down on the bed and touched his forehead to June's. "He made you perfect, you know that, exactly how you should be."

June sniffled.

The Devil wrapped an arm around him. "Say that for me. How did He make you?"

"He made me perfect."

"And I'm so glad He did," the Devil said. "I'll stay until you're asleep."

"Thank you."

"Happy Halloween."

"You hate Halloween," June said.

"You would hate it too if every morning after you had three dozen new black cats tearing up your room," he said, "Did you know that? That the sacrifices go right to my bedroom? Horrible. Babies are the worst, waking me up with their crying. Everyone sacrifices babies and cats, no one ever sends me a nanny or a pet sitter."

June didn't mean to laugh, but he did, an odd giggle that escaped without his permission.

"I don't know what they think I want with them..." he sighed.

June nestled against up him and closed his eyes; in his king's arms, hearing his heart and his nose filled with the smell of his skin, June fell asleep in no time.

JAMES KELLY did not come back. June had not expected him to. He took off the sheets and turned the pull out back into a couch. He took all of the vampire's things and shoved them into a closet, but he didn't think he would be back for them.

He went out to Long Island to visit Sissy as he'd promised and Wei came over at least once a week for a month to check up on him. He also sent over Micah a few times and June took comfort in the young man's arms.

That afternoon, after June had pulled himself out of bed, showered and dressed, the phone rang.

"Hello?"

"June, that you?" Wei asked.

"Yes. And you can't come over," he said.

"Hey, now, I'm just checkin in. I'm not gonna leave you alone—"

"I have plans."

"Bullshit you got plans. Wif who?"

"Kathy."

"Who?"

"The pregnant woman who called you yellow."

"Right. Don't say hi for me, then," Wei said.

"I won't," June promised and hung up. It was a lie, he'd already gone to visit Kathy that week, but he wanted time to himself without Wei or Peggy checking on him, without Marie offering to track the vampire down.

He pulled on the motorcycle boots he'd bought on a whim and searched around for the bomber jacket he'd acquired in a trade between himself and a soldier who wanted a family. June had given up on gray flannel wool; he had been wearing six different suits that looked almost exactly the same for years now. He had started wearing blue jeans and hanging out in smoky bars that smelled of old beer, surrounded by young men with greased-back hair who liked rock and roll and motorcycles.

This concerned Wei to some degree and June had laughed it off, saying "You're just worried that I'll stop hiring people from you."

"At least I know my boys are safe and clean. I worry about you."

"Don't," June had said.

He looked around for his keys and found them on the coffee table; he grabbed them and patted Gordon's belly for a few minutes before he left.

He ate lunch at his usual diner, not in the mood to cook for just himself, went to the store to buy soil and larger pots for some of his plants and returned home. He spent the remainder of the day peacefully repotting his leafy friends.

His life had settled blandly into a pattern of running errands, checking in on clients and doing housework. He didn't mind it, much, and refused to admit to anyone that the only thing missing was companionship.

As he lounged on the couch with his feet on the coffee table, watching his new television and picking the dirt from under his nails, the phone rang again and he debated whether or not he wanted to answer it.

After half a dozen rings, he reached over and picked it up. "Hello?"

"Junius Thomspon, you are a *liar*," Wei said.

"Maybe I'm tired of you babysitting me!" he said. "I'm going to hang up of you don't give me another reason why you called."

"My neighbor's cat had kittens."

"Gordon wouldn't like another cat around," June said.

"Yeah, but d'you want to come look at 'em?" Wei asked.

"No."

"They're all wee and fuzzy."

"I'm not going to Queens at ten at night to look at kittens," June said.

"It's nine forty-eight and Jackson Heights is *not* that far."

"Wei," he sighed, "What are you so worried about?"

"You've been moping around for a month, I mean, how many plants have you repotted?" Wei asked.

"They *need* to be replanted, it's not moping."

"Since that vampire—"

"Not him again! I don't want to hear about him or anything to do with him."

"*I meant* since you ripped that woman's throat out," Wei said. "Clearly you got somefin on your mind."

"I'm hanging up," he said and returned the phone to the receiver. He turned his eyes back to the television and Gordon jumped up on his lap. "What do you think, do you want a new little friend around?"

The cat sank his claws into June's thighs, kneading vigorously.

"Ouch, no, I didn't think so. I don't think my plants would survive another cat anyways." He stroked the cat on his head, down along his spine and Gordon arched his back against the caress.

He fell asleep on the couch and woke with a sore back. He puttered around in the morning, making breakfast and then heading out to Long Island to visit Sissy. When he arrived, she hugged him and made him sit for two and a half hours to see all the spells she had learned since coming to live with the Winston family.

He stayed for lunch and after that went for a walk around the neighborhood with Sissy and Gracie, who stopped every few minutes to sniff along the edges of the sidewalk. The walk took a long time and when he returned, Paula told him that Sissy spent hours every day taking these slow walks with the dog.

"She talks to Gracie more than she talks to us," Paula said.

"Animals are easier," June said with a shrug, not worried at all. "Teach her magic for animals and she'll be a wiz in no time."

"Neither of us know anything about husbandry and we don't have anything for it," Bob said.

"I'll see what I can find for the next time I visit," he said and glanced at the young witch. "Did you hear that?"

She looked at him and nodded.

"Then what did I say?" he asked.

She looked around, then shrugged.

"I said I'm going to bring you magic books for animals."

"Magic for animals?" she asked.

"You got it. Next time I come."

"Promise?"

"Promise," he said.

She grinned and turned her attention back to the dog.

He left before dinner and was back in his apartment by seven; he ate leftover Chinese that he shared with Gordon, wondering if it would make the cat sick.

DECEMBER 23, 1953

PEGGY AND June walked back from the movies; they had gone to see a Rita Hayworth film together, without Marie, who didn't care for Rita Hayworth or Peggy's fondness for her.

"Do you think she'll still be upset when you get home?" June asked.

"If you come in for a drink, she'll have to pretend to be civil," Peggy said. "You are coming in for a drink?"

"Sure, I don't have anything else to do."

"Christmas plans?"

"Going to go to Long Island and drop off that book you found for me."

She nodded. "And for New Year's?"

"I was going to stay in."

"Nonsense, I'm having a party," she said, "You can't stay in."

"At your house? Won't it bother the rabbits?"

"No, not at my house, of course not," she said, "I did send you an invitation. Have you not been reading your mail?"

"I've been looking at it."

"Oh, June," she sighed.

"Don't," he warned, "Or I won't come in for a drink. How is Ginger's litter?"

"Very well, so far," she said.

Once inside, Marie looked at him and crossed her arms.

"Staying for a drink?" she asked.

"Unless you're going to look at me like that the whole time," he said.

"No, I don't care."

"Have a seat, June, I'm going to put on something more comfortable," Peggy said.

He went to the living room and sat on the couch; Marie followed him and after a quiet moment, he said, "You're being foolish."

She glanced at him. "I didn't ask."

"But I'm telling you. It's a movie. So she fancies Rita Hayworth, you're the one she lives with."

"Stop preaching," she said.

"You two have something good—"

"And you haven't got anyone at all, I don't *want* your advice."

He looked away from her and sat stiffly on the couch, blinking back tears and trying not to rub his eyes or chew his nails. By the time Peggy returned, he had started to gnaw on his thumbnail.

"June, don't, this city is so dirty," she said.

He pulled his hand away.

"I'm surprised you're not sick all the time," she said, handing him a drink.

He took it, sipped it and said, "I don't get sick much."

"Must be one of the perks of being handmade by God," she said.

He gave her a small smile.

She turned on the radio and then came to sit beside him on the couch. "You've been going to those rock and roll bars."

He shrugged. "I like the music. Are you going to see that new Marlon Brando movie with me?"

"You just *went* to the movies," Marie said.

"*The Wild One*," he said.

"Are you going to come to my party?" Peggy asked.

He rolled his eyes. "Of course I will," he said. "Are *you* going to come to the movies? I hate going alone."

"Of course I will, I think Marlon Brando is a good actor."

Marie mumbled something to herself.

"You're invited, too, Marie, you know that," he said.

"I don't want to go. I hate Marlon Brando," she said.

"No, you don't," Peggy said.

"Don't tell me what I like," the fairy snapped.

"Uh, maybe I should go," June said.

"No, stay, so I'll *behave* myself," Marie said, giving Peggy a dirty look.

"All I did was go to the movies with a friend," Peggy said. "I don't know why you get like this."

"Probably has something to do with being fairy, addled my brain," she said.

"God, not this again!" Peggy said.

"Please stop," June said, feeling his chest start to ache.

"We are all the same, aren't we?" Marie asked Peggy.

"Please, girls, don't," June said.

Peggy looked at him and asked, "June, are you crying?"

He nodded, wiping his eyes.

She came closer to him and offered him a kerchief. "Why on earth are you crying?"

"I hate it when you two fight," he said.

"June..."

"Now we aren't even allowed to fight?" Marie grumbled.

He sniffled and said, "I'm sorry it's just...if you two can't make it work, shit, I don't know. I'm sorry."

"June, what are you talking about?" Peggy asked.

"I love you both and I want you to be happy," he said, "And I'm scared that if you leave each other you'll make me pick sides."

Marie snorted. "That's stupid. We were friends before anyways."

"It's not, you can't even let her go to a Rita Hayworth movie without being nasty about it!" June said, "What will you do if I told you I had lunch with your ex?"

"You're shouting," Peggy reminded softly.

"Sorry," he said and wiped his face some more. "It's just, I haven't got a lot of friends, you know, just you two and Wei and Sissy."

He thought about Micah and wondered if he could call a prostitute he paid for affection a friend; about as much as he could call Gordon a friend, he decided. Neither had any choice but to spend time with him.

"You've got more friends than that," Peggy said.

"None that I see," he said.

Peggy sighed at him as though he were a child and said, "Everyone likes you, June, you're being maudlin."

"Mawkish," Marie agreed.

"I can't help it."

"I don't think you try very hard," the fairy told him. "Humans like to be sad."

"I'm not human," he said.

"No, but you act like it," she said.

"Do not," he said sourly.

"Well, you don't act like a demon."

"Ugh, and what are we supposed to act like?"

"Oh, well, considering the Obliteration, I'd say demons act like vicious monsters who like the feel of fairy blood on their hands," she said.

"Not that again!" he said. "It's not my fault you all came in trying to do *our* work."

"Whoever said it's your work?" she demanded. "Fairies have just as much right to make deals."

"Fairies don't make deals, they grant wishes," June said, "There's a difference."

"Don't start going back and forth about this again," Peggy said wearily. "I can't listen to another debate between deals and wishes."

"Fine," June said, "But fairies grant schiesty wishes."

"Demons," Marie spat.

"Finish your drink and wipe your face," Peggy told June.

He brought the glass to his lips. "December thirtieth, that's when the movie's coming out," he said. "You're both invited."

"Why have you been wearing blue jeans lately?" Peggy asked.

"I don't know, I'm sick of suits," he said.

She shrugged. "Just curious."

He took the last sip of his drink. "I think I'm ready to go home."

Peggy took his glass and said, "We'll have to do something more fun together soon." She gave him kiss on his cheek and saw him to the door.

Marie followed him out and said, "I know you're not that type of demon, though. And I don't hate Marlon Brando."

He smiled. "I'll see you."

She nodded and waved as he walked out.

DECEMBER 31, 1953

JUNE SPENT Christmas with the Winston family, giving Sissy the book he had promised her, and on the thirtieth, he went with the girls to see *The Wild One*. On New Years' Eve, he pulled on a pair of jeans and wondered if Peggy would be disappointed that he hadn't dressed up for her party.

He double checked the invitation she'd sent him and took a taxi to one of the mansions on 5th Avenue; as he stood outside, he felt underdressed for a moment, but ignored it and went inside. It was barely ten o'clock but within he found a party in full swing. Someone checked his invitation, then directed him towards the bar with the friendly reminder, "Drinks are, of course, on the house. Happy New Year, sir."

"Thanks," he said.

He ordered and looked around for a tip jar, concerned for a moment until he saw that an elegant vase was being used instead. He tossed in a dollar, took his drink and began to wander around. He wondered if he would be able to find Peggy at all in this mess.

He ran into at least a dozen people he knew as he wandered from the bottom floor to the top; none of them knew where Peggy was either though at least half of them had seen her, so he felt better to know that she was there. On the top floor, he spotted Marie in a ludicrous silver lamé catsuit that he imagined she had stolen from the set of a science fiction movie.

"Marie, what the hell?" he asked as soon as she came over to greet him.

"At least I'm not wearing dungarees to a party in a mansion."

"But I look good," he said.

"And I don't?" she asked.

He glanced her over again. "I'm sorry, I can't take you seriously in that," he said.

"I think it's beautiful."

"Fairies, all the same, I hope nobody left out any cream and honey," he said.

She smacked his arm but smiled as she did it.

"Where's Peggy?"

"She's around somewhere, I think she went to get another drink, or maybe something to eat."

"There's food?"

"Sure, somewhere," Marie said. "There's waiters going around with trays. Look, there's one." She said and pointed.

"I'll be right back," he said and chased down the waiter, uncouthly taking a handful of small quiches.

When he returned to where Marie had been, she was gone, so he stood in place and ate his quiches, slowly and thoughtfully, looking around for someone else he knew. He didn't spot anyone, so he abandoned his empty drink glass and went back to the bar.

The clock behind the bar told him that it was half an hour until midnight; he wondered if he would have anyone to kiss when the year turned.

"I remember when no one ever knew what year it was," a man who had also come to the bar said to him as he waited for his drink.

"Hmm?"

"Back when I was young, we had no idea what year it was. It was just time to plant or time to harvest," the man said. "Or time to freeze."

"Right," June said, "I remember."

The bartender placed his drink before him and he took it, wandering back off, only realizing after several minutes that the man may have been doing more than being conversational. He didn't know if he should double back or continue to float through the party, but before he could decide, he spied an open chair and beelined for it, but a couple tumbled into it, entangled and giggling. He sighed and turned his eyes away.

A whisper went through the party and it turned to clamor;

midnight was approaching. People grabbed on to each other, their drinks moving often to their mouths, their hands running along the hands and arms and backs of their partners.

He scoffed when the countdown began and winced at the uproar when people cheered the stroke of midnight; the clocks' chimed and people kissed. June abandoned his empty drink glass again and decided that if he couldn't find Peggy on his way back towards the entrance, he would leave.

He followed the wall around the room, trying to find a doorway that wasn't crowded with people; he wanted to avoid pushing through any crowds. He brushed accidentally against a pair of young men pressed against the wall and muttered an apology, then did a double take.

Once he realized who he had brushed against, he laughed gleefully and heartily.

The couple turned to look at him and he said, "Sorry, carry on."

He turned to go, but James Kelly grabbed him angrily by the shirtfront and June flinched. As the vampire pulled him closer, he grew worried and tried to pull back, putting his hand over the vampire's to pry his fingers off his shirt.

He froze when James Kelly kissed him hard, biting his lip and then pushing him back, still holding onto his shirt. June didn't know what to do and couldn't catch his breath; he felt like he'd been hit by a train, in the best way possible.

"You stupid monster, you were supposed to come after me," the vampire told him.

"You shouted at me. I thought you wanted to be alone. Or away from me, at least," June said, feeling like he might float away if the vampire let go of him.

"When someone storms out, you're supposed to follow them!"

"That's something they made up to sell tickets to dramas."

"No, it's romantic!"

June laughed and wrapped his arms around him, hugging him tight. "You beautiful thing, I don't think I've ever loved a human so much."

James Kelly melted into his arms and said into his shirt, "I'm not human."

"Oh, but you are, as human as they come."

The vampire grinned up at him and June noted that his fangs had finally grown back all the way.

The handsome young man he'd been kissing cleared his throat and James Kelly glanced at him, smiled and said, "Happy New Year."

"You too, I guess," the young man said and walked away, looking as confused as June felt.

James Kelly said, "You're taking me home tonight."

"I am?" June asked, very surprised.

"Yes, I've been staying with my parents and I can't stand it anymore. My mother keeps trying to make me *eat*."

"Your parents!"

James Kelly nodded.

"Do I get to meet them?"

"They accepted vampires well enough, I don't think horned blue demons will be any worse," James Kelly said, reaching up to touch June's horns. "Am I allowed to touch these? I mean...it's not...?"

"No, you can touch them, it's fine," June said, coming to his senses and realizing that the vampire was very drunk, on alcohol and blood. He could smell both on his breath and it made his heart sink a little.

"They didn't care for Annie."

"What about me being a man?"

"I came back from the war alive, or mostly, I don't think they care. They'll worry, of course, but they worried about me being seen with a white woman."

"You're very drunk."

"Yes."

"You have glitter in your hair," he said, reaching up to brush sparkles from his curls.

"Someone was throwing it around." He kissed June again, wrapping his arms around his neck. "I want to go home now."

"Right now?"

"Yes."

"Alright," June said and checked to make sure he had his keys. He kept an arm around James Kelly as they walked out. "What are you doing here anyways?"

"Peggy said I had to come, she found me at my parents and made me promise."

"Of course she did."

"She said...she said that she wanted me to know the community better, to, uh, not to think that Annie was what all vampires are like. Is Peggy a vampire?"

"No, not really."

"Not really?"

"She's a blood bond," he said.

"Oh."

June kept a firm hold on him, especially on the stairs. As they entered his apartment and James Kelly collapsed on his couch, he asked, "Are you moving back in?"

"I'm allowed to, aren't I?" he asked, propping himself up.

"Sure."

"Come here," he said, holding out his hand.

June took his hand and the vampire pulled him onto the couch, on top of himself, and June straddled him carefully, making sure not to crush any tender spots. The vampire kissed him a lot, pressing his lips to his throat and untucking June's shirt so he could run his nails along his back.

June pulled away from his kisses and took his hands, holding them together between their bodies.

"What?" the vampire asked.

"What are you trying to do?"

James Kelly flushed, pulled his hands back and, sounding a little angry, said, "Trying to have sex with you!"

"You're very drunk."

"So?"

"So you get this way when you're drinking," June said. "I won't do it if you're drunk."

With a tremble in his voice, he asked, "What if I have to be drunk?"

"Then we won't."

"Ever?"

"Never."

"Then you won't want me anymore," the vampire accused. "You won't be with me if don't sleep together."

"I'll love you anyways," June said. "It doesn't matter if we fuck. I don't care."

"Liar."

"If you have to be drunk to do it, then you're not ready. And I don't want you to ever do something you're not ready for."

James Kelly looked so unsure that June thought his heart would break; he embraced him and kissed his curls. "We can talk about in the morning. Let's go to sleep."

June stood and stepped towards his bedroom, not knowing if James Kelly would follow him, but he did. He pulled off half his clothes and threw them on the floor and looked up at June as he changed into pajamas.

"I like you in jeans," the vampire said.

"Thanks. Do you want pajamas?"

"No."

"It's cold and the heat isn't great."

"Ugh, fine," he said.

June tossed him a pair of pajamas and the vampire pulled them on without getting up. He wriggled under the covers and pressed close to June, wrapping his arms around him and holding tight.

"What's gotten into you?" June asked.

"I love you."

"I hope so."

"What's that mean?" James Kelly asked, pulling back to look at him.

"Tell me again in the morning."

"You don't believe me."

"You're drunk and you spent the better part of the last year telling me off for being one of those dangerous homosexuals. Who was that boy you were kissing?"

"What? I don't know. I didn't...it was only a kiss for New Year's."

"Have you been kissing lots of handsome young men?"

He sat up and cried, "No!"

"Shh, don't shout, I'm right here," June soothed, "I'm just asking what you've been up to since Halloween."

"Does it matter?" he asked, bristling.

"Oh, I don't care if you've been kissing people or sleeping with them or giving five dollar hand jobs in alleyways," June said, "Don't tell me, it doesn't matter."

"I wouldn't do that," James Kelly said.

"Come here, lay back down," June said, putting an arm around the vampire once he had settled back into bed. "I won't ask you what you've been up to, I won't even ask what made you decide you could love me, too."

James Kelly stayed quiet and June thought he must have fallen asleep until he said, "I wanted you to follow me so bad. I thought...if you followed me, I would know that you really wanted to be with me. I waited, you know, for a while, smoked a whole pack of cigarettes."

"Why didn't you just tell me how you felt?"

"Because I *couldn't*. Every time I ever tried to say anything, I choked."

June turned his head and yawned into his pillow. "Sorry, I'm sleepy, but I'm listening," he said, but James Kelly didn't continue speaking. June fell asleep wishing he could feel happy about what had happened.

JANUARY 1, 1954

JUNE EXPECTED to wake up alone and when he saw that James Kelly still slept beside him, he expected the biggest meltdown yet when he woke up. June reached out and touched him on the arm, giving him a small shake.

The vampire pushed his hand away.

"Are you hung over?" June asked.

"Yes," the vampire said into the pillow.

"Do you remember last night?"

"Shut up," James Kelly said, covering his eyes.

June got up and, taking sprigs from some of the herbs in his apartment, brewed a hangover remedy and brought it back to the vampire.

"Sit up and drink this."

James Kelly sat up and held his hand out.

"It's hot, be careful."

He sipped at it and winced. "Tastes bad."

"It works, though," June said. He sat on the bed and watched the vampire sip from his mug, waiting nervously for him to realize where he was and react poorly. James Kelly said nothing at all, though, and June started to worry. "Do you want breakfast?"

"I've got to go to my parents, I told them we would do brunch," he said.

June nodded. "Do you think we can see each other sometime

soon?"

James Kelly looked up.

"It doesn't have to be like last night, but I want to see you."

"Come with me."

"Are you joking?"

"No."

June grinned. "Going home to meet Mom and Dad. This is quick."

"Too fast?" James Kelly asked, his face clouding instantly.

He shook his head. "No, not at all."

They sat in silence for a while until June asked, "Do you feel better?"

"I'm not going to throw up, you can stop staring at me."

"That's not why I'm staring."

"Then what?"

"I'm waiting for you to tell me off about last night," he admitted frankly.

"Tell you off for bringing me home, keeping me safe and not letting me do something I was too drunk to do?"

June nodded.

"No. I know I'm rotten sometimes. I meant it, with everything I've got, when I said I love you. As a friend, as something more."

"That's all I want," June said. "Can I kiss you?"

"I'm going to taste like this horrible tea."

"I don't care. Can I?"

"Yes."

June leaned in and kissed him. "Do you want to take a shower with me? It's not as fun as it sounds."

"Uh. I, um..."

"Say no if you don't want to."

"I don't know."

"I'm going to shower, come in if you change your mind."

The vampire nodded.

June went and after about three minutes heard him come in and say, "I'm just brushing my teeth."

"That's fine."

June started to wash his hair and heard the vampire ask him something, but couldn't hear exactly what it was thought the water. "What?"

"Uh, never mind."

"No, tell me."

"Maybe I could come in?"

"Sure you can," he said and pulled back the shower curtain at the end where the water sprayed less.

He peeked out and saw James Kelly standing there, naked with his hands covering himself between the legs. June grinned and the vampire flushed. June extended a hand and James Kelly took it, not looking him in the face as he stepped over the edge of the tub and into the shower.

James Kelly stood hesitantly for a little while until June had finished washing his hair and edged towards the vampire, saying "Switch with me, your turn to get wet."

As James Kelly stood under the shower, June took the bar of soap and the washcloth and lathered it up.

"What...uh."

"Oh, no," June said, "I didn't mean to mislead you. Bathing is very important to me, when I say take a shower, I mean take a shower."

"Oh."

June reached out and touched his arm, stepping a little closer. "I mean, I'm not opposed to fooling around a little bit."

James Kelly smiled a little, putting his hand on June's forearm.

"Come on, I'll wash your back, turn around."

"This is your idea of fooling around?"

"I meant I'll wash your back and touch your butt," he said, turning the vampire around, wrapping one arm around his waist and kissing his shoulder. "Or not, I don't care, tell me what you want."

He stepped back a little, still keeping his hand on James Kelly's waist, washing his back, covering his beautiful brown skin with suds and watching them wash away. He moved his hand lower on his body, gripping his hip lightly and brushing the washcloth across one butt cheek.

The vampire nearly dissolved into giggles. He turned around and put a hand on June's chest, looking over his body; his mouth tugged down after a moment.

"What?"

"You've got a lot of scars."

"Sure, and my nose is crooked," he said with a shrug. "Broke it too many times."

"What happened?"

"Lots of things that I don't really want to talk about," he said.

"Don't make that face, it's not tragic, just boring." He dabbed the washcloth on the tip of James Kelly's nose.

He washed the vampire and James Kelly washed him though they both doubled checked their more private and ticklish parts to make sure they were really clean.

They dried and dressed. June pulled on a pair of jeans and James Kelly eyed them. "What?" June asked. "You want me to wear a suit?"

"No. I told you I like them."

"You're not worried about what your parents think?"

"You have horns, I don't think the jeans will be what they notice," James Kelly said.

"True enough," June said. "Do you want to wear something of mine or get your things out of the closet?"

"You kept my stuff?"

"I thought about throwing it down the trash chute, but that seemed drastic," June said.

James Kelly walked out and came back with a box of his things. "All wrinkled, though," he said, looking through his clothes.

"I've got an iron," June said, reaching into the box and taking out a pair of trousers. He went to his own wardrobe and took out a burnt orange sweater. "Here, you should wear this."

James Kelly shook his head.

"Yeah, come on, I bought it because I like the color but it looks weird with my skin. People don't consider that some of us are blue when they design clothing. Or trying to find a hat I can wear with my horns? Impossible!"

He pressed the sweater into the vampire's hands.

"Are you dressing me now?"

"I've been thinking about you in that sweater for months," June told him. "I've been thinking about books you should read and things I want to buy you and what movies I want to go see with you."

"Are you fucking kidding?" James Kelly asked.

"No. Too much, I guess. I'm sorry to say you'll find I'm very domestic."

"I never got past hoping I'd be able to say how I felt and a kiss."

June reached out and touched his cheek. "Wear the sweater, we've got a brunch to go to. Do we know what's on the menu? I'm hoping...shit, no bacon, huh? Let's go, get dressed."

James Kelly shook his head.

Half an hour later, they took a cab to the Rosenburg home in Brooklyn. The vampire hesitated outside for a moment, then took out his keys and let himself inside.

"Is that you, Mouse?" a woman called from the kitchen.

"I brought someone with me," the vampire said, rubbing his eyes.

A woman came out of the kitchen, her arms crossed. "What do you mean you brought someone with you? Who? Not someone you picked up at some party."

"Momma," James Kelly said.

"What, him?" she asked, looking at June, unimpressed. A man came from the kitchen as well and eyed June's horns.

"This is June," James Kelly said.

"June? June who helped you with that trouble you were having?" she asked. She looked at June more fully and asked, "Are you the one who gave me my son back?"

"Was he missing?" June asked..

"Wouldn't eat, didn't drink, never came out in the daylight! He was a ghost. You fixed that," she said.

"I just helped," June said. "He did all the hard work." He glanced at James Kelly and gave him a big smile, totally enamored with and very proud of him.

He noticed the vampire's parents exchanging a look after he smiled at their son.

"Is there something you want to tell us?" his father asked, clearing his throat and touching his tie.

James Kelly's face went pale and he started to shift.

June frowned because he had sounded so confident the last time the subject had been brought up; of course, he been high on blood and drunk then.

"Leave it alone, Harry, he always tells us what we need to know," his mother said.

"Uh, anyways, June, these are my parents, Harold and Elizabeth Rosenburg," James Kelly said.

June smiled and said, "Nice to meet you." He took a chance and held out his hand to Harold, who reached out to shake it and then hesitated, looking at his claws.

Harold drew his hand back.

"Yeah, claws, sorry," June said, "I'm very careful with them, though."

"Sure."

"Alright, get out of the foyer, come into the kitchen, the food's just about ready," Elizabeth said and returned to the kitchen.

Harold walked away without looking at his son or their guest. James Kelly tapped June on the arm and said, "This way."

June took his hand and squeezed gently, saying softly, "You're doing good."

James Kelly started to pull his hand back, but stopped and squeezed back. He nodded and walked with June to the dining room.

"Mouse?" June asked as they sat down.

"I was shy," James Kelly said with a shrug. He had not sat next to June, but on the other side of the table and one chair down. June tried not to dwell.

"And quiet. Never got a peep out of him," his mother said, coming out with a casserole dish and setting it on the table.

She held out her hand towards June and said, "Your plate."

"Thanks," he said and handed it to her. He thanked her again when she handed it back.

Once they all had their food, she looked at her son and said firmly, "Now, you eat that."

"I don't *need* to eat."

"You *like* French toast," she told him and turned her eyes to June. "Tell us about yourself. What do you do?"

"I, uh." He hesitated and looked at James Kelly, who gave a small shake of his head. "I'm sort...a midwife, I'd say."

"And the horns?" Harold asked.

"It's a fertility thing," June said.

The man pressed his lips together and didn't say anything else.

"Um, I know they look sort of...well, he hasn't even got horns, you know."

"Who?" Elizabeth asked.

James Kelly shook his head again, but June said, "The Devil. Everyone thinks I've got horns because of the Devil, but he hasn't even got them."

"June, please," James Kelly said quietly.

"It's a new trend anyways, no one used to think he had horns. No one used to really care about him that much. Christianity is *much* more concerned with hell and Satan and all that."

"June."

"Eat," Elizabeth said to her son. "You sound like you know

what you're talking about when it comes to this. Do you do a lot of reading?"

"I was around. I'm old."

Harold asked, "Around? Before Jesus?"

He nodded. "Long time before him."

"What are you?" Harold asked.

June felt James Kelly's eyes boring into him and shrugged. "Just one of those creatures, I guess."

"I can't imagine," Elizabeth said, "Never having any idea about all this."

"We try to leave you alone as much as we can."

"Really?"

"Mortals and the undying don't mix very well; we fall in love, make friends, have kids...then someone dies, it's all very tragic," June said with a shrug. He added after some thought, "Of course, it doesn't always work out that way. And it is hard to stay away from so many people. Humans are everywhere."

"How interesting," Elizabeth said.

Harold said nothing.

June tucked into his breakfast; he had not eaten since that handful of quiches last night. He tried not to notice the quiet that grew around him, heavy and uneasy. He finally looked up at James Kelly, who had not eaten, and glanced at the vampire's mother, who stared at her son.

"You should try it, it's good," June prompted.

James Kelly looked at him, his lips pressed tight together.

"You don't need to eat, but you can still taste things," June said, "It's polite and it helps you blend in better."

Sullenly, the vampire took a single bite of his breakfast. "It's good."

"Thank you," his mother said.

A few more minutes passed and his father asked, "Where'd you get that sweater?"

"Harry," his mother scolded.

"What? I've never seen it before and it's *not* what he wore out. Am I not allowed to wonder when my son comes home in a sweater I've never seen before?"

"I borrowed it," James Kelly answered.

Harold looked towards June, then turned his eyes away.

"It doesn't go with my sort of blue," June said, "I mean...maybe for decorating, but not for being a person."

Harold cleared his throat and June figured he didn't know what to say.

"It's a lovely sweater," Elizabeth said.

"Thanks. Food's good."

"Thank you. This one's some sort of breakfast casserole, I got the recipe from one of the neighbors and figured now was a good time to try it."

He nodded and he glanced around the apartment a little more. Questions occurred to him and he decided not to ask them, especially because, as he looked at the food before him, he recalled that drinking blood was definitely not kosher.

"I, uh," James Kelly said and they all turned to look at him. "I'm not going to be living here anymore."

"What?" his mother asked.

"I'm moving back with, um, to where I was before."

"Where were you before?" Harold asked. "You wouldn't tell us. Just with a friend, that's all you ever said."

June sipped his coffee and looked at James Kelly.

"Manhattan," James Kelly said, not looking at June.

His parents looked at June.

"I'll still visit," the vampire said.

No one spoke; June heard the clock tick fifty-three times before Harold asked, "Isn't June a *woman's* name?"

"Dad," James Kelly hissed.

"Figure it might be," June said.

"You parents named you that? A girl's name?"

"My father named me Junius," June said, "Most people just call me June. I don't mind either way."

"Still..." Harold said.

"Still, I wouldn't want to be associated with women, not considering how feeble and dull they are," June said. "They're just the worst, can't stand them. It's why I decided to only sleep with men."

"Don't go putting words in my mouth," Harold said.

"It's what you meant. It's what everyone means," June said.

"Please," James Kelly said.

"Harold, leave it," Elizabeth said firmly to her husband as he began to open his mouth, "Don't go picking at people's names and expecting them not to take it the wrong way."

James Kelly left the table.

"Where are you going?" Harold asked.

"More coffee," he said. He returned a moment later with a hot cup and spooned sugar into it.

"All that sugar's not good for you," his mother said.

"I don't think I need to worry about it," he said, setting the sugar spoon down with a clack and picking up the one he used to stir. He stirred his coffee for a long time and June watched, wondering what he had been like as a child.

"Were you always this grumpy?" June asked.

The vampire looked up. "I'm not."

"You are a little bit."

"He was," his mother said, "A little raincloud sometimes. It was always...about two weeks into school, we would get a call from his teachers about him fighting with the other children."

"Mr. Rosenburg, I can't believe it," Harold said, imitating a teacher's voice, "He's so *quiet*, I never expecting this from such a nice little boy!"

Elizabeth laughed.

"But the other kids learned not to pick on him," his father said, giving his son a small, proud look.

June wanted to say something sweet, to ask who would ever pick on a lovely thing like him, but he kept it to himself.

"Any luck looking for a job?" Elizabeth asked.

"I think it's time to go," James Kelly said, standing up. "We'll come back for Purim."

"I was only asking," his mother said, "Sit back down."

"When you say *we'll* come back...?" his father asked.

"I mean June and me," James Kelly said, still standing. "That's...just going to be how it is now. Both of us or neither of us."

James Kelly's face flushed and he clenched his hands together.

"So if you don't like it, I'll really go," the vampire threatened after neither of his parents said anything.

"I like him better than that white woman you were hanging around with," his mother said. "He eats."

June smiled. "I do eat."

James Kelly pressed his lips together.

"People are gonna give you trouble," his father warned.

"People give me trouble anyways just from looking at me or hearing my last name," James Kelly said.

"Sit down," his mother said. "June, do you want more coffee?"

"Oh, you don't have to get up, I can—"

"No, no, you sit," his mother said. "Give me your cup."

June gave her the cup, but when it was time to clear the table he insisted on helping clean up and elbowed James Kelly in the back as he didn't help. "Come on, lazy bones, help out."

Elizabeth brought plates to the sink and June said, "You go sit down, we'll take care of it."

"No, you're a guest," she said.

June looked at James Kelly, who said, "Momma, go sit, I've got it."

"You sure?"

"Yes."

She patted his cheek. "You're such a good boy."

Once she left the kitchen, June came behind James Kelly and wrapped an arm around his waist, burying his face in the crook of his shoulder. "You're so brave," he said softly.

"Shut up," the vampire said, but it sounded insincere.

June put his other arm around his chest and squeezed him tight. "I love you."

"You too."

"Do you want to wash or dry?"

"What?"

"The dishes."

"Dry."

June released him, rolled up his sleeves and turned on the sink. He washed all the dishes contently, his head filled with stupid ideas about what his years to come would be like with James Kelly.

After they finished the dishes, they stayed for a little while longer until James Kelly made an excuse to leave. He hugged his mother and father goodbye and June even got a handshake from Harold.

When they stepped outside, James Kelly tugged his hand out of June's grip. He stayed about six inches away from the demon the whole journey home.

"Are you mad?" June asked.

"No," the vampire answered.

At home, June asked again, "Are you mad at me?"

"I told you I'm not."

"You seem upset."

"No."

June watered his plants and made sure Gordon had food. He tidied around the house and finally stood before James Kelly, who had settled into the couch with Gordon on his lap, and asked, "Are you embarrassed to be with me?"

He looked up from his book. "What?"

"You wouldn't hold my hand."

"I don't want to get the shit beat out of me," he said frankly.

"Oh."

"Yup."

"I won't let anyone hurt you," June said.

"You can't really promise that."

"But I'll try as hard as I can."

James Kelly looked down, then back up at June. "Is it wrong to be scared?"

"Of course not." June sat beside him. "I meant it when I called you brave." He kissed his cheek.

JANUARY 8, 1954

JUNE FELT like a predator. Every night for the past week, when it was time to settle into bed, James Kelly had frozen up, looking scared. More than scared, June decided, he looked deer-in-the-headlights petrified.

It happened as they changed into pajamas; he would look at June as though he might attack. June had once made the mistake of trying to kiss him when he was frozen like that; the vampire had flinched away from his touch.

"What is that you think I'm going to do to you?" June asked once they had changed into their nightclothes. James Kelly had sat on the bed and at the question, he looked up.

"What?"

"When it's time for bed, you freeze up, get all nervous."

"I don't know I guess...I'm sort of used to, when we got ready for bed...Annie and I would usually...I know you're not her, I know that, but..."

"But bedtime was when she pounced?" June asked with a smile. "And you think I'm going to pounce, too?" He sat beside the vampire.

He nodded.

"Did you like it? Being with her?"

He nodded again.

"But you look worried."

"I...I'm scared it will hurt."

With growing concern, but wanting to confirm his suspicions, he asked, "That what will hurt?"

James Kelly shook his head but answered in a small voice, "Sex."

June rubbed his eyes.

"I heard...the other guys in my units, they said what guys would do to each other in bed. They got pretty...you know, graphic in the descriptions."

"And were any of them gay?"

"I don't know. I don't think so."

"So maybe don't believe what they told you."

James Kelly nodded, sheepish.

"Poor dear," June said, touching his shoulder.

"Stop, I'm not as pathetic as you think I am."

"I don't think that at all," June said, "I think you're sweet and lovely. And maybe a little angry."

"Maybe a little."

"But I think you're perfect."

"Shut up."

June pulled him close and buried his face in the crook of his neck. "It feels right."

"What?"

"Holding you. It feels like I should have always been doing this."

James Kelly clung tight to him and kissed his throat for a long time, pressing his lips to the vein in his neck. "You smell nice."

"Aftershave."

"No, underneath it, your skin, all of you, has this smell. It's not the way that humans smell. It's...warmer. Richer." He took June's hand and pressed his mouth to his wrist. He traced his tongue along the vein there, then pulled back. "I'm sorry, I..."

"I wouldn't mind. If you asked," June said.

"Your heart sped up."

He smiled. "I'm excited."

"To...for me to bite you?"

"Yes."

"Why?"

"I've never let anyone take my blood before, but all those times watching you drink from people...you were so...*involved*, you looked so abandoned to it." He reached out to touch James Kelly's face, running his thumb along his cheek. "Will you bite me?"

"I'll hurt you."

"I trust you," June said. He kissed him, holding him by the back of the head. The vampire pressed back against him, pushing him onto his back.

"Do you really want me to?"

"Yes."

"Where?"

"Anywhere you like."

With nervous hands, James Kelly touched June's throat, then rolled up the sleeve on his pajamas. "Here?"

June nodded.

"I don't have my timer."

June laughed and kissed him. "You don't need it."

James Kelly kissed June's forearm, twice, then opened his mouth. June felt his teeth press lightly into his skin for a second; the vampire was hesitating.

"Go ahead," he said.

James Kelly looked up, then bit into his arm, carefully. A sharp gasp slipped from June's mouth and the vampire's grip tightened on his arm; June took it as a comforting gesture. The vampire's mouth on his arm was tender and June reveled in the small noises of pleasure that James Kelly made.

The feeling of blood being pulled from his arm was strange, but not unpleasant. He did not keep count in his head, but James Kelly pulled back sooner than he had expected.

Breathing quickly, the vampire said, "Your blood...it's...it's like the way you smell."

"I was handmade by a god," June said with a smile.

James Kelly touched his arm. "Do you need a Band-Aid?"

"No, it will close soon."

The vampire reached over to the bedside table and pressed a tissue over the two small wounds. He kept his hand there and June put his hand over the vampire's. James Kelly scooted closer to him and June wrapped his other arm around him.

"Are you sleepy?" June asked.

"Yes."

"Goodnight."

"You don't want anything?" the vampire asked, nestling his cheek against June's chest, running his hand down June's side to rest on his hip. He pulled June's hips towards his.

"Ohh, so handsy when you've had something to drink."

"We could."

"I thought you were scared."

"You said I was brave."

"You are brave," June said, "Can we be brave in the morning?"

"You really don't want to sleep with me at all, do you?"

"I want it to be right," June admitted sheepishly. "Is that silly?"

"I don't think so."

June kissed his hair and pulled the covers over them. "Besides, there's lots of things we can do before we get to that."

James Kelly's grip on him tightened and he pressed his mouth to June's. "I'm sorry I couldn't do this sooner. There's so much time to make up for."

"We have forever. I'm not in a rush," June said. "Goodnight."

"Night."

With the vampire nestled against him, June fell asleep, wondering how long this could last; he didn't know, but he hoped it would last forever.

About the Author

Dan is a writer and educator who has lived in or around Wolcott, Connecticut for their entire life. They received their BSED from CCSU in 2013 and is currently writing their Master's thesis on representation of women in same-sex relationships in contemporary Spanish literature and cinema.